Zonta survived the Turn Over at Gentle Acres, a communal project she helped design alongside her late husband. Her life as a master gardener is fulfilling, but she feels something is missing. The answer comes when a Protector enlists her to keep an eye on Jake, an agent of the Authority. Zonta can't deny her attraction to Jake, but can she love an enemy while protecting all she holds dear?

Jake decides his assignment to the wasteland of Gentle Acres is more than worthwhile the minute he sees the beautiful and exotic Zonta. When he tours the commune and meets the people, he is certain the peaceniks have nothing to do with the two agents he is searching for. As Jake learns truths he never knew, he concludes that perhaps his dedication to the Authority is wrong.

Can Jake prove himself to the Protectors and his new lover? Can Zonta risk losing her home and another lover to the Authority?

Where The Bodies Lie
Copyright © 2021 Cindy A. Matthews
ISBN: 978-1-4874-3385-7
Cover art by Martine Jardin

Published by eXtasy Books Inc.

Look for us online at:
www.eXtasybooks.com

Where The Bodies Lie

By

Cindy A. Matthews

DEDICATION

This story is dedicated to those who fight for freedom everywhere, of all kinds, in all times and places.

CHAPTER ONE

Zonta scanned the ripening corn swaying in the midsummer's breeze as the blazing sun edged below the western horizon. The earthy scents of growing things made her smile. *Gentle Acres* was indeed a fitting name for what they had created collectively out of the aftermath of chaos.

They should feel pleased with their efforts. Zonta felt immense satisfaction, considering all the obstacles and setbacks she and her neighbors had overcome in the last decade. The communal garden was by far the most successful project she had ever been a part of or had ever hoped to be involved with. It was all the more bittersweet since she had taken the journey alone.

I wish you could be here, David. It's what we'd dreamed of doing oh-so-long-ago when we were young and naïve, and the screwed-up world seemed to hold the slightest possibility of redemption. Too bad the Turn Over put an end to our dreams, huh?

"Earth to Zonta! Earth to Zonta!" Jenna called out from the fire pit area. "We're about to start the bonfire. You coming?"

"In a minute," she shouted back. "I have to do the nightly check off first."

"Okay, but don't be too long. Elise really wants to try out her new marshmallow recipe along with our chocolate substitute and Daphne's homemade graham crackers."

"Hmm . . . Sounds great."

Zonta hopped off the rusting tractor seat and headed toward the small aircraft hangar they now used as a communal barn and storage facility. They all had come a long way from the early days of horror and deprivation. Her garden helpers deserved all the summer fun possible not declared illegal by the Authority.

Zonta shuddered. *They'd have to catch us first. But what isn't illegal for us lowly Have Nots? We're fortunate the Haves can't be bothered with our gardens and our bonfires and leave us in relative peace.*

As if the cosmos read her mind and its desire for tranquility, a familiar shadow crossed her path. She halted.

"Hello, Daniel. Long time since your last visit. What's up?"

"We have a favor to ask of you . . ."

Zonta groaned and threw up her hands. "Why am I not surprised? It's not like you usually come to help us with the crop harvesting or fruit picking."

She turned and stomped into the hangar-barn, Daniel following closely behind. From the unwashed smell that lingered in his vicinity, it was obvious he'd been on the road for some time. Sleeping rough, most likely, unless he'd been able to bunk at one of the neighboring communes in their region.

Daniel, the thin, scruffy twenty-something with haunting eyes and peach-fuzz cheeks, was the child she'd never had and probably never would have. They walked in silence past the various chicken coops and pens that held the community's small menagerie of livestock. She knew he wouldn't speak openly until they were inside her make-shift garden office with the door closed.

In the gathering dark, she turned on her solar-powered battery lamp and placed it on the old metal desk. Daniel looked unkempt and unfed as usual, adorned in a torn-at-the-neck t-shirt that was stained with dirt, sweat, and God knew what else. His threadbare-at-both-the-seat-and- knees jeans and duct-taped high-top sneakers completed the ensemble.

Zonta shook her head, but she didn't judge him, because his outfit was totally in keeping with post-Turn Over fashion for the Have Nots. Her own cut-off jeans and faded tie-dyed top possessed more patches than original cloth. It was high time they did some trading with the Scavengers for new clothing stocks.

An unusual air of nervousness about Daniel was apparent in his pacing. Zonta intuited that all was not well. She frowned and sat down at the desk.

After a few moments of mutually tense silence, she spoke. "Oh, come on and come out with it, Daniel. What's up? You're not one to beat about the bush."

"Funny you should say so, but I have been — beating about the bushes, metaphorically, as Daphne likes to say."

He paused his pacing and looked her straight in the eye. "We've scrounged up everything we needed to complete our *surprise*. The dream has become a reality."

"All of it?" Zonta raised an eyebrow. She hadn't really believed that what the Protectors had been scheming for more than a year was possible, but stranger things had happened in her lifetime. "So, it's set to go?"

Daniel nodded. "The shitty thing is that our friends to the North shared some intelligence with us, saying that the Authority could be onto us."

Relief washed over her. She sighed. "You're calling it off then?"

"Not necessarily. The Authority could be just acting out their usual paranoia. They may not make the trip as they planned, and all our recent hard work has been for nothing. So, that's where you come in. Your help might be necessary."

Zonta clenched her fists in her lap. "I thought you were going to say something like that. You want us to help out the same as last time, don't you?"

Daniel shrugged, his bony shoulders practically poking through the thin material of his filthy shirt. "Possibly. Word has it that the Agency is sending someone more knowledgeable, not someone like the complete bastards they sent before to check us out."

He leaned forward and rested his hands on the desk edge. "Do you think you could handle it? Keep the Agency off our backs while we work on the finishing touches? Make them think we're *friendly* natives?"

Zonta bit her lip. "I don't know. I won't know until I try. Does Jefferson know about this development? Any of the others on community council?"

"Nope and nope, but I'll talk to Jefferson soon. I'm not sure anyone else on the council needs to know. It's probably better that they don't."

"No kidding."

A cold frisson of terror rolled down Zonta's spine. She remembered how the members of Gentle Acres Co-operative Farm had been recruited to aid Daniel's cell several months back. What they'd been asked to do hadn't been what she had expected. When she'd first heard of the Protectors' mission to bring about peace and freedom, she'd assumed it would be just that—peace and freedom. Their defensive measures weren't exactly noble gestures, but she acknowledged that fighting fire with fire was sometimes necessary.

"You know, cleaning up after your messes can be pretty scary and morally repugnant at times," Zonta managed through gritted teeth. "Correction, they're *always* scary."

Daniel shrugged again. "Well, that's how you know they're worth it."

Zonta nodded. "Let's hope so."

I hope this mess involving the Protectors will be worth it, David. Otherwise, I might be joining you soon.

She stood and pushed painful memories into the furthest recesses of her mind. "You wanna stay for the bonfire? We have food, and you look as if you haven't eaten in days. Daphne will be there, too."

Daniel sniffed his armpits. "Not sure Daphne will want to see me looking like this. I'd better go and wash up first."

"You do that. It'll be appreciated." Zonta chuckled. "We'll see you in a little bit."

As silently as Daniel's shadow had crossed her path, he departed.

Zonta grabbed her to-do list from the desk and quickly checked off the day's tasks completed. Then she double-checked that the children had watered the chickens and piglets as she'd asked them to earlier in the day. Her work done, she closed the hangar-barn door and headed toward the bonfire to enjoy the fellowship of her gardening comrades.

Gentle Acres. It's not all that gentle whenever Daniel and his acquaintances are about, but maybe, just maybe, it'll be worth the risk this time.

CHAPTER TWO

Jake looked out the small aircraft window at the field below and blinked twice. Were those tall yellowish things *sunflowers*? He'd only seen them in photographs before. Usually, anything green growing in or around the Workers' Zones was dismissed as weeds and pulled and processed into ethanol for fuel.

"We're landing soon," his pilot and fellow agent, informed him. "Put your seatbelt on. It'll be bumpy. This old strip hasn't been maintained, so I'm assuming it's full of potholes."

Jake strapped in. "Surprising they've left this airport alone, considering its convenient location connecting the Have Zones on the coasts."

"The Haves figure that ramjets and pleasure blimps don't need much runway." His companion's reply had more than a touch of cynicism in its tone. "It's the complete opposite of what's needed for this type of plane. Or even the old crop dusters that utilized this particular side of the airport."

Jake gazed wistfully out the cabin window. "I sort of remember coming to an airport like this as a young kid. My mom had to pick up a family member who attended my father's funeral. She acted amazed anyone even bothered to show."

"Ah, those wild pre-Turn Over days and their lack of respect for our cherished elders." The pilot chuckled to himself. "Whatever did we do before we were blessed with the benevolent order and security we enjoy nowadays, thanks to the Authority?"

"Yes, all thanks and praise to the Authority," Jake murmured, careful to ignore the note of sarcasm in his companion's tone. He'd learned the hard way that it was safer not to acknowledge another Zoner's cynicism toward their rulers. Instead, he focused his thoughts on the verdant fields below.

This mission transported Jake back in time to when life started to make no sense. He was four years old when his father had died of a sudden heart attack. He couldn't even remember his father's face now. It had been so long. From what he could remember, work had always seemed more important to his father than building a relationship with his son. Sixty, seventy hours a week of work and more work, all so they could have a nice house and nice things to put into it. At least that was what his mother had told him when he was a little older, and they no longer possessed either a father-husband or a home. All that seemed to matter then, as now, was to work like a dog to get ahead, no matter how futile it was or how quickly it killed you.

"Pleasant surprise. Seems like the Authority completely forgot about this little airport—except to bomb it once or twice." The pilot snorted. "Lucky for us, they missed the runway I'm using."

Jake laughed along with his companion. In the Agency, it always paid to fit in. *Always*.

"Yeah, the land around here wasn't bombed like the inner city was. The natives have made good use of it here," Jake explained as the plane banked to come around to make its final approach. "From what I learned at my briefing, they've got twenty acres planted in food crops and are raising pigs, goats, and chickens."

"What a waste. If only they'd move to the work zones and do as they're told, they'd be taken care of with all the processed food they could eat." The pilot hit a switch to lower the aircraft's wheels. "Here goes nothing. Brace yourself."

Jake had to concentrate hard to keep his breakfast from escaping his stomach. The plane shuddered, pitched, and vibrated violently before rolling to a stop on the gravel-strewn airstrip.

"Whew. That was better than the last time I attempted a landing on one of these relics of the past." His companion grinned. "You got your communications device implanted?"

Jake pressed the flat-topped, mole-sized dot on the left side of his neck to be certain. The intra-ocular screen popped up in his field of vision, telling him his heart rate, blood pressure, and general health condition were within permissible limits and that he was connected to the Agency's communications satellite.

"I do," he acknowledged.

The pilot gave him a thumb's up. "You know how to contact the Agency for extraction then. Maybe they'll be able to fetch you in a helicopter if the bigwigs don't have them all in use like today." He reached over and swung open the door for Jake. "Good luck, Agent Gunderson."

"Thanks." Jake grabbed his backpack, double-checked his gear, and hopped out of the plane onto the cracked and pitted tarmac. "I'll be seeing you soon, Agent. I sure don't want to miss the playoffs."

"No, you don't. There are lots of folks who'll want to bet against your picks." The pilot laughed. "Close the door and get on out of here. Sooner you clear this hellhole of wrongdoing, the sooner you can come home."

Jake waved his companion goodbye and then turned and hiked toward a small grouping of trees. Within moments, he heard the plane taking off, leaving him at the mercy of the elements and the natives.

A large, abandoned hangar building stood not too far away. Perhaps he could make that his base of operations while he questioned the residents of the bizarrely named commune *Gentle Acres*. There was no way life outside of the Authority's control was *gentle*.

Upon closer inspection, Jake realized why the building and airstrip had been abandoned. A huge hole in the roof and a crater in the floor indicated it had received a *gift from above* — as the firebombs were called, deadly gifts the Authority had rained down upon the uncooperative populace during the early days of the Turn Over.

Among the dusty debris of civil war, there were signs of recent use, however. Several old vehicles were parked in one of the corners of the cavernous hangar. Spare parts for many more seemed neatly stacked alongside the walls that still offered some protection from the occasional strong winds and unrepentant heat of the summer sun. It appeared to be some kind of a workshop. But why would anyone be working on fixing up fossil-fuel-powered engines out here?

"There's a lot more to Gentle Acres than meets the eye," Jake said to himself. Not finding what he felt was a secure enough location to plant his signal booster, he decided to head toward a smaller hanger in the distance, closer to the sunflowers. For some reason, he really wanted to study them up close.

"Can I help you?"

Jake spun around and found himself breathless at the sight of a beautiful, statuesque woman standing three meters away from him. For the past few minutes, he'd been lost in observing the towering, almost human-faced flowers.

"Uh, yes, I mean no, I . . ."

The ebony-haired goddess, wearing a long, loose braid, flashed him a warm, inviting smile and took a step toward him, raising her open hands in greeting. "It's okay. Lots of folks get lost in the sunflower field while on a day hike. I take it you're from the local Workers' Zone?"

Close enough. "Yeah, that's it." Jake brushed the dust off on his pant legs. "I'm taking a hiking holiday."

"We don't get many visitors here, but you're welcome to tour Gentle Acres in the daylight hours as long as you follow the rules and don't harm the crops, livestock, or wildlife. We depend upon them to nourish us, body and soul."

Her smile continued to dazzle him. She appeared to be about his age—forty-something—but there was a timelessness and grace about her. She was the real thing. Every beautiful woman he had encountered up until this moment seemed manufactured and programmed like sex androids at a decadent Have orgy.

"If you have any questions, just ask any of the garden workers. My office is located in the building directly behind this field." The vision of loveliness turned to go.

Jake could barely form a coherent thought, let alone a sentence, but he knew in the core of his being that he couldn't simply let her walk away.

"Why do they call it *Gentle Acres*?" he blurted out.

She turned and laughed—a delightfully tinkling laugh like wind chimes—then approached him.

"Good question. It originally was just the name given to a subdivision of small bungalow-style homes built in the early nineteen-fifties next to what would later become the Metropolitan Airport. We've expanded the name to include our community gardens and orchards. Mr. Gentle was the house builder's name, and the land had previously belonged to a dairy farmer, hence *Gentle Acres* to give it a country feel. It was quite common to name neighborhoods like this during the post-World War II period to entice rural folks to move into the city. Or so I've been told by our resident historian."

Jake was still finding it difficult to formulate a decent question. But he didn't want the breathtaking brunette to leave, so he asked the first thing that came into his head. "You have a resident historian?"

"Yes, we have a historian and a historical society. We also have our own schools — kindergarten through college and tech and art schools. We have our own community orchestra and public library as well."

She narrowed her eyes and tilted her head as she regarded his response. "You're finding this all difficult to take in, aren't you?"

Jake nodded slowly. "A little. It's just that . . . we're not told much about life outside of the Zone."

She smirked. "Of course not. It's not advantageous for the Authority to let on how many survived the tear gassings, the gun massacres, the drone bombings, the forced labor camps, not to mention the epidemics that followed the so-called *peaceful* Turn Over. Not all of us gave up and gave in to the *benevolent dictator*. Some of us remained true to our ideals."

He opened his mouth to speak but found himself speechless under her barely concealed contempt-filled glare.

This woman is judging me. But what could I do about where I grew up? My mother dragged me into the Workers' Zone. It was that or starve, she said. Some days, after my drunk stepfather beat her, I wished she had let us starve . . .

"Those of us with a spine made it, and we're still here," the beautiful woman before him said through gritted teeth. "Now, if you'll excuse me."

Before Jake realized what he was doing, he reached out and grabbed her by the arm. "Can you at least tell me your name?" *I've never met a goddess quite like you — even if you don't approve of me or where I live or what I do for a living.*

She hesitated and sucked in a breath but didn't pull away. "All right, but only if you tell me yours first."

He released the breath he didn't realize he'd been holding. "Gunderson. Now you."

"We use only first names here. Mine is Zonta. I'm Gentle Acres' head gardener."

"It's nice to meet you, Zonta." He couldn't help but grin as he gloried in her fathomless dark brown eyes. "You have a lovely garden here. And please, call me Jake."

Zonta smiled and arched a dark eyebrow. "It's nice to meet you, *Jake*."

He moved his hand slowly down her forearm and clasped her hand. Her gaze met and locked with his. Her hand remained wrapped in his, and her breathing slowed. The sparkle in her eyes indicated she wasn't entirely averse to his physical presence.

"Could you possibly give me a private tour of Gentle Acres?" he suggested.

Zonta fluttered her long black lashes. "I thought you'd never ask."

CHAPTER THREE

Zonta allowed their guest to walk in front of her and set the pace of their tour. Jake seemed genuinely interested in Gentle Acres—surprisingly so. The greenhouse intrigued him. He couldn't get over how old windows and broken glass panes from the rubble of their city had been repurposed to construct something both architecturally beautiful and useful at the same time.

If only Jake wasn't working for a bunch of fascists. He's quite handsome for a white boy. Almost as attractive as you, David, if you don't mind me thinking so. Although his steel-gray eyes and the silver touch at his temples make him look rather like a wolf about to devour me whole. I miss your chocolate-colored eyes and skin, my love. Our children would have been even darker than us as we bred out the last of the European heritage from our bloodlines. Too bad we never got the chance.

The children's garden—designed, planted, and well-maintained by their youngest co-op members—took him off guard. Jake appeared shocked to see young children taking charge of their own food supply. It was almost as if he thought children weren't capable of making their own decisions and implementing them. He even got down on his knees to speak to the youngest gardeners, the pre-school group, as they worked beside their teachers and their older siblings. It was touching to see how gentle and eager he acted among them.

Zonta caught herself admiring Jake's backside as he bent over to help one little boy plant a tomato start.

Jake's got a great ass and a surprisingly muscular build for a denizen of the corporate plantation. Does he work out at the gym or whatever they call it? I suppose agents are expected to be in fighting shape at all times. He must realize that we've had plenty of contact with ordinary workers and can smell a cop on sight.

"Time for our afternoon snack, kiddoes," Cate, the kindergarten director, called out.

The little ones gave a communal squeal, dropped their hand tools, and ran over to the picnic area to enjoy fresh goat's milk and early season berries.

Jake stood and dusted the dirt off his canvas trousers.

Zonta momentarily turned her face away, confused that a man who held such a repellent job was a source of so much fascination for her.

"Where next?" He smiled.

Zonta chuckled. "You worked up quite an appetite. You want to enjoy snack time, too?"

Jake stuck his hands into his pockets and rocked back and forth on his heels. "Oh, no, that's all right. I don't want the children to be deprived of any of their food. I can wait."

"No problem. There's enough for everyone here. No one goes hungry."

The incredulous look he flashed her contained a mixture of intense sadness along with doubt.

"It's really okay," she assured him. "We're self-sufficient. There's no need for food rationing here like there is in the Workers' Zones, from what I understand."

Jake looked down at his hiking boots. "There hasn't been too much food rationing in the Zones since . . . since I was about these kids' age."

Her heart went out to him. "That must have been tough growing up there."

"You don't know the half of it."

"No, I don't." She took his hand in hers. "Maybe you can enlighten me over afternoon snack?"

They strolled hand-in-hand to sit at one of the tables beside the fire pit and watched the children standing patiently in line to receive their treat.

The more Zonta smiled at Jake to encourage him to ask questions, the more she realized she liked it. Sure, he was pumping her for information and learning the lay of the land, but wasn't she doing the same?

Jake can't help it that he is caught up in the Authority's grip. He seems hard-working, polite, and able to deal with the repressive culture he's stuck in with grace. He might be one of the lucky ones who are never tempted to pop pills to endure the endless monotony of serving the ungrateful Haves. I can actually picture myself waking up beside that somewhat boyish face with its permanently lost look and enjoying every inch of that hunky body. I've been rather lonely as of late . . .

Zonta shook her head, catching herself before her erotic daydream took precedence over her part in the mission. She knew better than to fraternize with the enemy. Still, she'd been charged by Daniel with sussing Jake out to see if he was a threat and keeping him occupied so he didn't wander too far. Continuing to play the friendly hostess was essential to those tasks.

And was it a crime to enjoy herself while doing so?

Several hours later, the sun began its descent toward the horizon, promising relief from the heat and humidity.

"You've been rather question-free since I showed you the *hügelkultur* mounds, Jake." Zonta broke the silence between them as they toured some of the oldest and shadiest areas of Gentle Acres. "Was my detailed explanation of how tree log composting and soil moisture retention aids in growing squash vines a bit too much?"

"It was on the technical side," he admitted with a smirk. "You know your stuff. Did you study it before . . ."

His words trailed away, but his inquisitive look filled in the blanks. Zonta didn't mind giving him a little of her personal history.

"Yes. I was studying ecology and urban agriculture at the university before your beloved dictator shut them down and started eliminating those who didn't agree with his assessment that *science is heresy* and *ignorance is bliss*."

Zonta bent to weed a small patch on one of the mounds. She observed Jake from the corner of her eye to gauge his reaction to another slight of the Authority that he served. *No nervous tics or grimaces. He doesn't seem overly attached to the regime or sentimental regarding their asshole leader. Good.*

"I'm glad you got to use your education the way you'd planned," he replied. "You've obviously been very successful, growing such a wide variety of crops and feeding so many people."

Zonta turned her head to assess his unexpected response, which seemed earnest. She rose and smiled. "Thanks. But I think you've missed the point. We don't measure success the way your society does. We simply serve the community to the best of our abilities. We vow to pass on our knowledge to others so they can do the same in turn."

"But you're proud of what you've accomplished at Gentle Acres, right?"

She shook her head. "Not proud like you're thinking. I'm happy to have passed my knowledge on to several others who have or will become master gardeners in their own right. My actions guarantee our people will be fed in the future. I couldn't have done it without the help of many others, however, so there can be no pride taken in this accomplishment alone."

"But the garden wouldn't be where it's at today without your leadership and guidance, is what I'm saying," Jake clarified. "That's got to make you feel proud." He thumped his chest. "You're the boss. I've noticed how the others treat you with respect."

Zonta laughed at his persistence. "We teach our children

16

manners and to respect all life—including gardeners. And pride isn't necessary or even wanted. As Brother Jefferson reminds us all constantly, *Pride goeth before a fall*. Our former country fell far and broke apart because of the pride and avarice of a handful of wealthy men, don't you think?"

Her attention fell to his full, sensual lips.

What would it feel like to kiss you? What's the worst that could happen if I tried? You tell me you're not into girls?

"Uh, you got me there," Jake finally responded.

Zonta backed away from the squash beds and motioned toward the trees. Jake followed her. She had wanted to be totally alone with him since she had first set eyes on him.

"What do you do in the Workers' Zone?" she asked innocently as they strolled toward the most secluded part of the orchard. "Don't tell me you're a farmer. Or do they call you *agribusinessnmen*?"

He laughed. "I wish I could be, but there isn't that much open space in the Zones. I do like the others do. I get up each day and do as the bosses tell me to do. They give us our pay at the end of the week, and we use it to cover our rent and expenses, and then we start all over again."

If it wasn't for that Agency-issued backpack and the high-quality shoes and clothing, you could very well pass as an average working stiff from the Zone, Jake Gunderson. You don't want to reveal your true occupation to me, but is that because you're sworn to secrecy or an indicator of genuine disgust for what it represents? Could you be longing for a way out?

Zonta shook her head and sighed. "Sounds monotonous. Don't you ever get bored or lonely living such a meaningless existence?" She stopped and leaned back against a tree trunk in the darkest area of the wood. "I know I'd go insane if I couldn't see the sky and the earth each day. How do we know we're truly alive if we don't experience life to its fullest?"

Jake took a step toward her, his gaze riveted to hers. "You're right. We should experience life to its fullest."

Zonta tilted her head and fluttered her lashes. "Do you really know how to experience life to its fullest, Jake?"

"I have a feeling there's a lot you can teach me on that subject," he muttered, taking another step toward her.

She slipped her arms about his neck and drew him closer. "Are you willing to become my pupil?"

He didn't answer in so many words, but Zonta knew Jake had accepted her proposal with no reservations. Their lips met, and together they lay down across the coolness of the earth, their bodies becoming one.

CHAPTER FOUR

"If this is how you treat every stranger who crosses your fields, you probably have captured quite a harem of workers by now," Jake joked.

Please tell me I'm the only man you've ever brought into these woods to be intimate with. I don't know why, but I want to be the only one.

Zonta shifted her weight slightly as she lay in the crook of his arm, staring up at the dappled light raining through the tree branches. She was slow to respond, as though carefully considering her reply.

"I've never done anything so . . . impulsive before. Please forgive me."

"There's nothing to forgive you for." He caressed her cheek.

"But I know how you Wanna-Haves are used to docile and proper-acting females. How does that old saying go? *Barefoot, pregnant, and in the kitchen is a woman's rightful place.*" She chuckled. "It can't be much fun if your partner is chained to a stove all the time."

Jake laughed. "I know I can't wait to try your cooking, if it's half as good as your *dessert.*"

He pulled Zonta on top of him, kissing her soundly. He couldn't take his eyes or keep his hands off her. She had curves in all the right places, and her long legs had enveloped him and pulled him even deeper into her eager recesses. At her age, he couldn't expect her to be a virgin. Perhaps she had a boyfriend or husband waiting somewhere nearby with a

19

pitchfork? And his weapon was in his backpack—wherever he'd flung it!

Jake was amazed at how off guard Zonta had thrown him when she'd enticed him into the woods and out of his clothes. Not that it took much persuasion for him to cooperate. It had been too long since he and Kellyanne had parted ways. He was hungry for sex and lonely for a woman's touch. He longed for feminine understanding and compassion. But was he so needy that he'd compromise the mission he was on?

Slowly, sadly, Jake pulled his lips away from his surprising new lover. "I hate to say it, but I don't think we can stay here forever."

Zonta sat up. "You're right. I have duties to attend to and chores that need doing."

She leaned over him and grabbed her thin, flowing caftan dress, bunched it up, and slipped it over her head. He was shocked and excited when he realized she didn't wear anything like the bulky undergarments women wore in the Workers' Zones. The sight of her dressing and the thought of her leaving his side any minute left him feeling forlorn.

"Can we . . . meet up later after you're done working?" He didn't want her to leave.

Zonta stood and slipped on her panties, then shoved her feet back into her work boots. She smiled down at him. "I'd like that very much."

"I'll meet you at your office in a couple of hours? That's the hangar with the animals in it?"

"We'd like to think of it as a barn, but it is a former airplane hangar."

"A good way to repurpose an old structure. Repurpose, re-cycle, reuse . . . What else did you say earlier?"

Zonta flashed that winning grin of hers. "Reduce, reuse, repurpose, recycle, and compost. I'm glad you were listening and not just watching my ass as I bent over to toss things onto the piles."

She smoothed her long locks back and then quickly re-braided her ponytail. "I'd better go now. Why don't you take a little nap?" She nodded toward his crotch and smirked. "Looks like you'll need some rest to get going again later."

"Sounds like a great idea." He grinned and stretched his arms as he repositioned himself beneath the tree. "I'll have sweet dreams here. You know, I may never want to leave this grove. Too many fond memories."

She blew him a kiss and winked. "Later."

Jake allowed himself a brief rest, waiting until he was certain Zonta was out of earshot before he sat up and gathered his clothes and backpack together.

"You've got to stop thinking with your cock and start using your head, Agent Gunderson," he muttered as he dressed. "The bosses aren't going to understand your way of making friends with the natives . . . One particularly beautiful native, that is."

Hell, it's my tactics that helped to foil that last plot against our glorious leader's life. The bosses trust me and my instincts. Bringing Zonta over to our side could result in some crucial intelligence to solve my fellow agents' disappearance. Besides, the Agency owes me for breaking up my relationship with Kellyanne. Working all those late nights kept us apart. Of course she'd look elsewhere for solace.

A thought of how groin-achingly sexy Zonta looked lying beside him beneath the trees brought an instant smile to his face. Maybe breaking up with Kellyanne was for the best? He was free to pursue other women now, no matter how frowned-upon extramarital affairs were in the Zones — especially with outsiders.

Jake checked his backpack and retrieved his pen-sized signal booster. A small patch of wildflowers at the base of the tree would hide it well. After his pleasurable afternoon activities, he was certain he wouldn't ever forget its location.

"All right, signal booster in place. Time to sign in with the bosses." He pushed the small mole on the left side of his neck to bring up his communications screen.

GIVE FIELD REPORT flashed angrily in big red letters.

Jake mentally typed in his first impressions of his mission.

Successful landing. Preliminary tour of the farmland shows no overt signs of radical activity, and natives seem friendly. They don't act too surprised to see an outsider, which could indicate previous contact with missing agents. Investigating further.

He checked his incoming messages, filed his daily expense report, scanned the news and weather warning headlines, and then clicked out of the com screen simply by rubbing his neck.

Jake slipped on his backpack, chuckling, then stood and marched out of the orchard. Zonta was one friendly native he couldn't wait to investigate further. But first, he needed to examine the lay of the land some more. Those long earthen mounds with vines growing over them—what Zonta called *hügelkultur*—seemed a good place to start.

The last field reports filed by the missing agents stated Gentle Acres was their last known location. They couldn't have been abducted by aliens from outer space. That was the stuff of old sci-fi movies and considered heresy by the Church of the Authority. The two agents had to still be here, or at least somewhere in the vicinity.

Jake had been briefed extensively regarding Agents Smith's and Davis's personal backgrounds and notable careers with the Agency and sincerely doubted either of them had gone native. He couldn't picture them pulling out their communications device, growing their hair long, and moving into a yurt with the native partner of their choice. No, he was certain they hadn't done anything wild like that. It was up to him to determine where the bodies were buried and then find and arrest the guilty party or parties.

Jake wasn't about to be fooled by the Garden of Eden parallels surrounding him. There was a serpent in Gentle Acres as well as fruit ripe for the picking. And there most certainly was an Eve, a temptress by the name of Zonta.

CHAPTER FIVE

"No, not again. We're not fighters, Zonta. We shouldn't have to lift a single hand to do their dirty work. Daniel asks too much of us — and particularly you. Tell him where he can go."

The determined look in Jefferson's eyes, along with the accompanied ultimatum, convinced Zonta their community council leader meant what he said. However, she also knew from past experience that the former minister would give in when he understood the stakes involved.

She put a finger to her lips, closed the garden office door, and motioned her guest to take a chair before perching on the corner of her desk. Even with the extra height afforded by her seating arrangement, Jefferson still somehow managed to tower over her.

"Calm down, Jeff," she said in her most quiet and soothing voice. "It's not what you think. This time it's a distraction mission. We've just got to slow the guy up so he doesn't put two and two together and come up with six before the *surprise* is ready. The materials have been gathered. Shaun has got the electronics together, and they're hoping this last dump of fertilizer will be all it takes to —"

"I know." Jefferson cut her off with a swipe of his hand. "I know what they're going to do with it. The only reason we've gotten away with this charade so far is that those idiots in the Authority believe we farm the same way they do."

"I know. We've been fortunate they haven't caught on to us yet. Daniel really knows how to cover his tracks."

"But after this . . . whatever it is . . . happens, we'll never be able to go back to life as usual, Zonta." Jefferson leaned forward and lowered his volume. "The Agency will send out its jackbooted thugs to pulverize our crops. They'll be after us night and day."

"Like they haven't been after us for the last quarter-century?"

Zonta crossed her arms, thinking sadly how little had changed since the day the bombs fell. "Remember what they did to our families? Remember your Tawny and Keisha, and my David? We have to take this risk."

She hopped down from the desk and knelt at Jefferson's feet, taking hold of one of his large, dark hands. "I know you're scared to lose more people you care about, but this could bring the downfall of the Authority. We could reunite the workers caught in the Zones with their loved ones on the outside. We could all live together in peace and harmony like you used to preach about. You could lead us all into a better future."

He shook his head. "You know I gave up preaching for good after they blew up my baby girl and my wife. And I know for a fact, Zonta, that you're not a believer. Not even in your ancestors' ways, like you say your daddy taught you. You don't believe in universal peace. You believe in only one thing—surviving."

She pressed his hands to her lips. "Is that so wrong?"

"No, it isn't." He smiled. "You really helped me out when I was grieving, and you made me a stronger man. You gave me something to wake up for in the morning and tasks enough to make me tired enough to rest easy at night."

Zonta laid her cheek against his thigh as he stroked her head. "You helped me rest easier, too. I thought I would go insane after I lost David. I enjoyed how you comforted me."

Jefferson laughed. "I enjoyed it, too, but we both knew our

age difference was going to be a factor. You deserve a younger lover."

A flashback of Jake and her rolling about in the orchard brought a smile to her lips. She wasn't one to kiss and tell and thought better than to share that information with Jefferson. "I don't know. I had a hard time keeping up, as I recall."

Jefferson pulled a blade of grass from her hair and then pulled back to look at her askance. "Hardly. But let's not get off-topic."

Zonta got off her knees and smoothed down her hair. She bit her lip to hold back a chuckle at his questioning look.

"We created Gentle Acres and saved our neighbors and then helped others save their neighborhoods and more throughout this region. We have a lot to be proud of," he said with a self-satisfied smile. "But you know very well the community doesn't deserve this risk. You know our people don't deserve this. You also know the Authority won't let us go unpunished when they find out what we're doing. They'll come down heavy on us—*all of us*."

The bombs could start falling again. Zonta hadn't thought through all the possible consequences if the operation didn't go as planned. *What else can we do to end this nightmare of injustice? Don't we deserve to live free? We can't live forever in the shadows.*

She sighed. "Then it'd better work, because you're right, there might not be another next time."

A knock at the door caused her to take a step back. "Come in."

"The goats have gotten into the carrot patch again," her master gardener student Elise announced as she entered. "We chased them out and wrangled them back into their pens finally, but I thought you should know. They ate a lot more than they should've. "

"Shit." Zonta sighed. "Our ever-hungry goats are getting on my nerves. We'll have to replant."

The sturdy blonde nodded. "Lucky for us, we have six months of summer at this latitude nowadays. Plenty of time for us to plant another crop. That is if we get the rain."

"Oh, the upside of global warming." Jefferson lifted his hands high as he rose from his chair. "Well, ladies, I'll be running along now and return to my hard work of shelving books."

Zonta frowned at him. "Hey, don't down yourself. You have an important job. You make a dent in those latest *donations* from the downtown expedition?"

He whistled. "That bookstore warehouse find was phenomenal. We'll be processing those books and other materials for years to come. We're planning to donate most of the duplicates to School Hill Farms to start their own community library. Who knows? We might just be able to revive the entire metropolitan library system."

"Didn't they destroy most of the public libraries in the . . . *you know what*?" Elise whispered.

"They did." Jefferson placed a comforting arm around the young woman. "You're probably too young to remember how lovely some of our library branches were in this city. But in time, we'll revive them all, albeit in different buildings and locations. Some day."

Jefferson escorted them both out into the sweltering late afternoon sunshine, then headed toward the gate through the memorial garden that led out into their neighborhood. Zonta followed Elise into the vegetable garden and noted the damage caused by the goats. Things hadn't been nibbled as much as she'd feared.

After giving Elise a few directions, Zonta decided to leave the replanting to her garden helpers and track down Jake. Somehow she sensed that he wouldn't have gone too far.

It might be pure arrogance and vanity on her part to think she could trap a man and entangle him into her web—or her way of thinking—so easily, so quickly. But the gamble was worth it. Her instructions had been to keep him interested, but not too interested, in the goings-on at Gentle Acres. Surely gaining his interest through the art of seduction stood shoulders above gaining it through the threat of violence?

Zonta had discovered what Daniel and the others were capable of the last time agents crossed their path. She'd make sure they wouldn't go too far this time. They could survive and thrive without an overkill of vengeance.

After a few minutes, she spied Jenna hoeing cabbages and stopped to ask her for a report.

"I've been following him from a discrete distance like you said," Jenna replied, nodding over her shoulder. "He's been behaving himself pretty good. I caught him in the berry patch munching on the blueberries, and I told him what we tell the kids. *You gotta pick a whole container first before we'll let you snack.*"

Zonta laughed. "Did he do it?"

"He did. Surprised the hell out of me, too. I gave him two containers just in case he felt inspired, and I think he's still picking." Jenna took a step closer to Zonta and lowered her volume. "Is he the same sort as our last two *visitors*?"

Zonta nodded. "Yes. But they've sent him in alone, so either they think he's twice as capable, or they believe we're half as troublesome."

A tear formed in the corner of Jenna's eye. She sniffed it away. "After what they did to our Ramon, I'd soon as turn this one into pig feed. I suppose it's not our decision, though."

"No, it's out of our hands." Zonta pulled her petite friend into a hug. "Nothing will ever make up for our loss, but we can't lower ourselves to their level. We have to be better than they are."

"You're entirely too forgiving, after what they did to your life, your husband." Jenna stepped back with a crooked smile, looking Zonta up and down slowly, obviously taking in the less-than-perfect state of her clothing. "I trust you know what you're doing, Zonta, and it'll be worth it in the end."

"It will be."

Shit, I have no real idea what I'm doing, but I'll keep going until I do. Or Daniel gives me another order.

"I'll take care of the checklist tonight so you can concentrate on our *guest*." Jenna turned to go, chuckling. "I'd better get back to hoeing the cabbage rows. Remember to scrub yourself with a loofah to get those grass stains off your knees."

Zonta blushed. "Thanks for the tip."

Am I that obvious? Jenna apparently knows exactly what I've been up to without me saying a thing. Jefferson didn't mention it when he plucked the blade of grass out of my hair, but I don't think he's altogether blind yet.

Zonta smoothed her caftan down over her knees and held her head high as she strolled past her fellow gardeners working steadily in the heat of the late afternoon sun. *My neighbors will understand my actions are for their good. They won't judge me. But I will judge myself harshly later. I have to. I can't allow a simple fling to destroy the world we've built.*

CHAPTER SIX

The sun shining behind the thin material of Zonta's flowing dress perfectly outlined her figure beneath it as she approached. Jake froze, swallowed hard, and almost dropped the container of berries in his hand. He realized he was enjoying himself for the first time in a very, very long time and letting her unfettered sensuality go to his head.

Another region of his anatomy—one that hadn't experienced any Authority-sanctioned enjoyment since the official dissolution of his relationship—seemed to be calling the shots. The Agency didn't look too kindly on agents who satisfied their animal lusts outside of marriage. But wasn't that what the occasional walkabout outside the Zones was for?

What the hell has gotten into me? Here I'm acting as if I were partying in the amusement district with an android sex worker instead of concentrating on solving this case. This isn't professional or safe behavior.

But it's more than that . . . I'm falling for her. I can't allow myself the luxury of feelings toward Zonta, no matter how beautiful, how exotic and enticing she is. It's dangerous.

Jake bit into another berry and savored both its juicy sweet taste and the image of the fascinating and sexy woman walking ever closer to him among the row of bushes. He cleared his throat and looked away, trying hard to take his mind off her body and refocus on his mission. A blackberry prickle brushed against his hand, causing him to step back from the stinging nettles.

Luckily, he was up-to-date on all his shots. They could

possibly still be passing one of the viruses in these parts, and intimate contact was one of the most likely vectors of disease transmission. Or he could be passing something deadly onto Zonta — who knew what sort of immunity protection organic vegetation provided?

He'd heard that the only reason the Haves actually traded things of worth for organic products was for testing. They wanted to catalog what the various fruits, vegetables, and meat tasted like before all of it was grown from stem cells in a lab dish or from one genetically engineered stalk.

It's a rich man's hobby, collecting and eating natural food. Never thought I'd actually be doing it myself.

"You look like you've been very productive since I last saw you," Zonta called out in a husky voice.

The sound sent a shiver of anticipation down his spine.

"We could really use you as a picker in another week or so when the rest of the crop is ripe." She stopped, picked a blueberry, and popped it between her full lips. "Hmm . . . good, isn't it?"

Jake nodded. "It's very good."

Before he knew what he was doing, he put the container down and rushed toward her. She threw her arms about him and returned his kisses and eager caresses with even more of her own.

After several moments, she pulled away. "I keep forgetting there are children in the vicinity." She giggled. "We need to be more discreet."

He raised an eyebrow. "So says the woman who pulled me into an orchard and ripped off my clothing earlier."

She shrugged. "I got caught up in the moment."

"I'll say you did." His stomach chose that moment to rumble loudly.

Zonta smiled. "What a horrible hostess I've been. All you've had to eat today is blueberries. We must rectify that." She turned away from the bushes and set off down the path between.

Jake picked up his container of berries and followed, trying not to spill his harvest while keeping up with her brisk pace. "I ate some power bars, too. I never go anywhere without some in my backpack."

The low rumble of an approaching thunderstorm caused Jake to stop in his tracks. He scanned the horizon and spotted the raincloud rapidly approaching from the south.

Zonta turned around and shook her head at him before continuing on. "Your stomach sounds dreadful—just like your power bars do. Full of GMOs and artificially flavored goodness, I bet."

He hastened his steps to keep up with her. "The calories keep me going is all I know and care about, but they don't taste nearly as good as these blueberries, I'll give you that."

"I would think not. From the advertisements I've seen of the foodstuffs available in the Workers' Zone, I know I'd starve within a week. Explains why so many of your lot leave and wind up here."

"You've seen our advertisements? And what do you mean *others* leave the Zone?" Jake frowned. "Hey, wait up!"

Just as they cleared the berry patch and reached an open field, a sudden cloud burst rained heavily upon them. Zonta laughed and lifted her hands high above her head.

"I love it!" she cried. "Saves on shower water!"

From all corners of the garden, workers ran out into the open field. The younger ones spun around and around while their elders danced together among the rapidly falling droplets. Jake headed for the overhang of a nearby tool shed.

"Come on and dance in the rain with us!" Zonta shouted.

He mopped his brow with his bandanna. It was difficult for him to hear her over the hoots and screams of the children. So many children! There had to be at least a dozen. The natives here were as fertile as their fields. The kids seemed to find the downpour every bit as exciting as the adults.

"It's just rain," Jake shouted back at her. "It does it now and again in the Zone, too. We have storm drains to carry it away when it's too much."

"What a waste. Don't you collect it? Use it to water your crops or at least your flowers?"

Jake squeezed himself further under the shed overhang, but he couldn't keep from being soaked by the dripping from the eaves. "I give up. It looks like I'm going to get wet."

Zonta rushed forward and grabbed his hand, pulling him out into the melee of rain dancers. Within moments, she had him whooping and hollering, jumping in and out of puddles, and twirling her about.

After five minutes, the frenzy was over. The crowd slowly dissipated, chuckling and smiling at each other over the state of their disheveled hair and mud-splattered clothing.

Oddly enough, Jake found himself hoping it would start raining again. He couldn't explain the pure joy he felt at having the freedom to run about in the rain like a madman. It was as though he'd never been truly alive before this moment. The water falling from the skies had baptized him, refreshed him, and revived his soul.

Be careful there. This sort of thinking could be construed as heresy by the bishops of the Authority. Get serious, Agent. You have a job to do.

Jake cleared his throat and averted his eyes from the delicious outline of Zonta's curves scarcely hidden beneath the thin wet material of her dress. He found it difficult to fight off the urge to pull her into his arms and kiss her, audience or not.

"I take it you all don't see much precipitation?" he asked.

Zonta bent over to wring the water from her caftan hem, affording him a long look down her cleavage, before standing tall and answering him.

"There's not been much rain this summer so far. We've had

to rely on our water reserves to avoid tapping into the sub-standard Zone supply."

"You're getting treated water from the Workers' Zone?" He frowned. "How is that even possible?"

She grinned. "It's possible. We have a lot of smart community members. We also use the Zone's antique sewage network, such that it is. But our composting toilets produce a useful product we can use on our crops, so we're weaning ourselves off that route."

"But how can you access the Zone's—"

"Come along." Zonta smirked and motioned for him to follow her. "Let's get some supper and change out of these damp clothes. I'll have to come back later and finish up my checklist, but there's no reason for us to catch a cold in the meantime."

Jake struggled to keep up with the sexy vision in clinging material leading him to who knew where. The water squishing inside of his hiking shoes drove him almost around the bend, but he soon got into the rhythm. The intensity of the pop-up storm had surprised him, but the natives seemed to take it in stride. He worked inside most days, and the Zones he frequented had little in the way of open fields or even greenery. How would he know if this kind of rain event was a common occurrence?

It seemed no one in the Authority had bothered to keep records of climate activity since the 2020s. It wasn't important to the leadership. Obviously, nothing natural was important to them. The more Jake thought about it, the more he realized how only things that were manufactured ever seemed to generate their leaders' enthusiasm or gain their attention.

The sheer variety of plants and trees and people he'd observed in these last few hours had made him feel as if he'd landed on a remote, alien planet. It was so foreign to the gray, claustrophobic Workers' Zones of his home.

Why does the Authority call these Have Not communities shitholes? They're strange people, and they clearly don't respect the

Authority, but it's not all bad. They have children who don't appear deformed or sickly. The viruses and toxins obviously haven't affected their birth rates or chromosomes as they have in the Zones.

"This way." Zonta halted at an arched wooden gate covered in lush green vines and purple trumpet bell-shaped flowers. "I'll take you to my place through our Memorial Garden. We have to keep this gate closed in order to keep the goats out. They enjoy snacking on the occasional bush too much."

Zonta pushed the gate open and nodded for Jake to enter first. Normally he'd hesitate and take out his scanner to search for any heat signatures on the other side of the fence that could indicate a human presence preparing to attack. But the scents of long ago remembered flowers enticed him to proceed.

Jake stepped into the enclosed garden and stopped. All he could do was stand, frozen, marveling at the splendor of row after row of abundantly blossoming rose bushes. Their sweet fragrance overwhelmed his olfactory nerves. He felt dizzy and off-balanced.

"It's beautiful, isn't it?" Zonta closed the gate behind them and came to his side. She breathed in deeply. "Ah! If there is a Heaven—which is a totally irrational concept to me—then this is what I'd imagine it would be like. Yes, Heaven would be exactly like Madison's Memorial Rose Garden. Shall we take a short stroll?"

The perfume of roses must be a drug. I feel light-headed. No wonder we only are shown pictures of them, and they're only grown in the Leaders' Zones.

"Can we?" Jake managed after a moment. "I mean, isn't this area meant for only the leadership?"

Zonta looked at him askance. "If you have a pulse, you're considered a *leader* here."

They strolled in and out among the rows, the paths lined with narrow stepping stones. Small plaques and stones

35

painted with names and symbols appeared in between and in front of flower displays and mature trees. Jake remembered walking through a much larger, yet similar, sort of place when he was very young, a place called a *cemetery*.

Zonta halted in front of a flat rock with an unfamiliar symbol painted upon it in red. She sucked in a jagged breath as though experiencing a great loss over again at that moment. Jake realized now what this walled-in flower garden and the plaque lying in front of her represented.

"There is a Heaven," he murmured. "They taught me that from the first day I stepped into the Workers' Zone. I don't suppose you're a believer?"

Zonta shook her head. "No, never have been, but there have been a few who have tried to convert me. The bombings at the time of the Turn Over were pretty much the last straw for me to believe in a merciful and loving God."

Where have I heard that argument before? Oh, yeah, my mother used to say something similar whenever I asked her why we moved into the Workers' Zone.

"If an almighty, omnipotent being ever existed, it should have stopped the violence right then and there," Zonta continued, staring at the encircled *A* symbol on the rock. "But it didn't, and the violence continues to this very day."

Jake frowned. "No, we've been at peace for the past two decades. The Authority hasn't been at war with anybody."

She snorted. "Is that what they've been telling you? I suppose they wouldn't tell the workers in your particular zone what's happening in the other zones. Or in other parts of the world, for that matter. You all might not care for it. It's easier to keep you in the dark."

He nodded but didn't follow her train of thought. "Yeah, sure."

Zonta has to be mistaken. She could be confusing the past with present reality. Although, living outside of the direct control of the Authority, the natives of Gentle Acres might possess a clearer understanding of what is happening across the globe than I do.

Jake noticed then that she was shivering. Whether it was from the damp or deep-felt emotions, he couldn't be certain. He put an arm around her shoulders, trying his best to be of comfort in a situation he had little experience with. Death had become such a common occurrence in his culture that most mourning rituals had faded into memory. The bodies were simply taken away, and the families were informed their family member was now in *Heaven*.

"You lost loved ones during the Turn Over?" he asked.

"Didn't everyone?" she snapped. "But our loss doesn't define us. Living does."

"Wise words."

Zonta turned abruptly into another row, heading for a side gate, quickening her pace. "Yes, David said those words to me quite often. He was wise beyond his years."

Jake raised an eyebrow. *David?*

She flung open a rounded-top gate and entered a somewhat smaller walled garden. This collection of flora emanated strong, earthy smells, a mixture of sweet and savory scents. Jake felt his stomach rumble with hunger once more.

"This is our community herb garden, and this" — she nodded toward the back of a one-story cottage with dingy white siding —"is my place."

Jake followed Zonta up a few steps to a small patio area and then straight through a windowed door into a kitchen. No antique lock or card key. She didn't seem worried about her home being completely open while she was away working in the fields.

An unsettling thought passed through his mind. *Is there really no crime here? A utopia with a fruitful garden containing a beautiful woman and innocent children and roses . . . and no crime? Well, perhaps not petty theft, but possibly murder?*

"Take your wet shoes off and place them here on the tile."

Zonta switched on an overhead light and sat on a chair at

a small dining table, motioning for him to do the same. "On second thought, I think it's best to remove all our wet duds in here. Tomorrow's my wash day anyway."

Jake sat and struggled to untie his wet shoelaces. "You have electricity. Do you borrow that from the Workers' Zone as well as the sewer and water?"

"No, we create plenty of our own clean energy through our community solar panels. You may have noticed the panels on the rooftops when you flew in."

"If I knew what to look for, possibly. What's a solar panel?"

Zonta sighed. "I forget the Authority is still running small nuke plants. I'm surprised you guys don't glow in the dark."

She stood and removed her wet caftan dress in one smooth movement, then her panties, and tossed them into a basket in the corner before flouncing out of the room and returning with two towels.

Jake would never grow tired admiring the sensual woman before him, but business was business. He turned his gaze away to clear his head. "Did you say *flew in*? How did you know how I got here?"

"It's not a mystery. The plane engine made enough noise, even if you did approach the old landing strip from the north."

Zonta tossed him a towel and pulled hers across her nakedness, blotting out his perfect view.

"We've seen plenty of air traffic here," she continued. "The Haves used the commercial airport terminal for years, the runways beyond those huge warehouse hangar remnants. We used to be a hub for a large package delivery firm back in the day."

Jake finally kicked off his hiking shoes. "You seem to know an awful lot about this area long before the Turn Over began."

"We have a resident historian, remember? And I've lived in Gentle Acres since I came to live with my aunt to attend high school before college and . . ."

Zonta's face darkened momentarily but brightened when Jake stood and shrugged out of his wet clothes. She allowed her towel to slide to the floor as she approached him, flinging her arms about his neck.

She smiled. "Supper could wait a little while, don't you think?"

CHAPTER SEVEN

Zonta curled herself against Jake's strong, muscular back and sighed. With her eyes closed, she could pretend she had made love with David and not a complete stranger.

A stranger who stood for everything David had despised and warned her about.

A stranger she had been charged to watch closely. To become intimate with only if necessary to discover his mission objective and keep her friends and fellow gardeners safe.

Is it so wrong if I enjoy myself while accomplishing such a worthy task? After all, we're supposed to love our neighbors as ourselves, right? Isn't that what Jefferson preaches to the community whenever there's a disagreement? Love is the answer, and violence is never the right answer, he'll say. It sounds good, but perhaps both in equal measure are necessary for us to survive in this world?

"Zonta," Jake muttered. "Wherever did you ever get such a unique name?"

She sat up and allowed him to roll over to face her. "It's Lakota for *trustworthy*. My parents must have thought I was a trustworthy little girl when they gave it to me."

"Very interesting." He pulled her closer and kissed her for a long moment before pulling back. "Are you trustworthy?"

"I'd like to think I am." Zonta sighed and stretched. "Jake . . . That's a common enough name. However did you get it?"

He chuckled. "I have an ancestor named Jacob, so that's probably where it comes from."

"Boring story," she teased, "but it makes sense."

"What can I say? I'm a boring, poor, white kid whose mother never had an original idea in her life. Maybe she hoped I'd be as successful as her great-great-uncle or whomever she named me after. To this day, though, it hasn't come to pass, but I'm told if I keep working hard, I'll get there. Eventually."

Zonta caressed his cheek and smiled. "Keep believing the propaganda — it's what the Authority expects. You don't ever want to disappoint them."

Jake snorted. "Yeah, you don't want to do that. They can make it very difficult for you if you're a disappointment to them. *Very* difficult."

Zonta furrowed her brow. *Is he saying he has personal experience of crossing the line and antagonizing those in the Authority? Perhaps this job is his last chance to impress his superiors in the Agency . . . What will happen to him if he returns home empty-handed?*

"Is that you in the white leather dress with the beads and fringe?" Jake interrupted her musing. "The photograph on the opposite wall?"

She gaped in surprise. She hadn't thought about putting it away temporarily or that he'd even notice it.

"Yes, that's me." She turned away from his penetrating gaze. "It's our wedding portrait."

"You look happy. The tall, dark, and handsome man standing next to you is your husband?"

"Yes." She slid over to the edge of the bed and stood. "I don't know about you, but I think it's time we made supper." She grabbed a t-shirt and some old cut-offs out of a clothes basket in the corner and quickly dressed.

Jake sat up. "It's okay if you don't want to talk about it."

She nodded, then grabbed her hairbrush from her dresser and brushed her hair furiously to undo some of the tangles. She couldn't look at him. There were some things probably better left unsaid if she was to gain his trust.

"I'll assume he's no longer in the picture," Jake said in a quiet tone.

Zonta slowly put down her brush and turned to face him. Maybe some things should be said after all?

"David was killed in the first round of drone bombings on the city. He was a graduate assistant teaching at the university and a leader during the student uprisings against massive student loan debt, endless war, income inequality, police brutality, no access to health care . . . Shall I go on?"

Jake flinched slightly. "No, I understand. Is he buried in the Memorial Garden?"

She narrowed her eyes, closely observing his reaction. "Madison is the only one buried there, since it was her home and her idea for the garden. She passed away seven years ago. The others memorialized there . . . Well, we have no idea where the bodies lie. Like millions of others, there's no knowing what became of them. David disappeared in the destruction of the university. He and so many others like him simply vanished from the face of the earth that day."

Jake shifted his weight uneasily. "I get it. I'm sorry he didn't live to see things get better."

"Better?" Zonta laughed and walked out of the bedroom. "*Better?*"

When she reached the kitchen, she grabbed the first thing out of the cupboard — homegrown vegetable soup canned last summer. She opened the jar and was stirring the contents into a saucepan when Jake entered the room wearing nothing but the towel across his hips.

"Sorry I can't dress for dinner. My clothes are still wet."

"Oh. I can get you something else to wear. Just a minute."

Zonta set the soup to simmer and headed to the storage closet in the spare bedroom. She gathered up an extra-large t-shirt and some unisex drawstring pants still in their wrappings and tossed them at Jake as she re-entered the kitchen.

"Thanks." Jake caught them deftly and stared at the yellowed plastic packaging. "Wherever did you get these clothes? They look ancient."

"Scavengers dig up thousands of perfectly preserved items from the rubble of abandoned stores and warehouses all the time. We trade our veggies and fruits for them. I recently traded a surfeit of butternut squash for those things in your hands, as well as several hundred other pieces of clothing that were distributed throughout the community."

He frowned. "These say they're men's clothing on the label. Is there something you should tell me?"

She laughed. "No, I didn't get them for a male currently living with me. I just happen to like loose-fitting clothing, so they should fit you fine."

Jake ripped into the plastic wrap, brittle with age, and retrieved the t-shirt. "It looks like my size, and I do look good in dark blue. Thank you."

Zonta turned back to her dinner preparations. "Great. If you need any underwear, there might be some boxers in that pile in the other room you're welcome to try on." She paused at his bewildered expression. "Don't ask. Women's undergarments are somewhat rare in these finds."

"Explains why you like getting out of them." He winked.

"Right you are. Why don't you go ahead and take a quick shower? I have hot water — solar heated."

Zonta breathed a sigh of relief as he left the kitchen for the bath. She needed a moment alone to collect her thoughts.

Practically accusing Jake of being the cause of David's death might not have been such a good way to gain his trust after all. He might not disclose the details of his mission if she blew up in his face whenever he spouted the Authority's propaganda. She needed to keep a lid on her emotions.

Zonta busied herself with dinner preparations. She sighed as she considered how difficult it would be to make Jake understand how the Authority wasn't making the world a better place.

Before and during the so-called *bloodless coup* of the Turn Over, the junta of oligarchs had forced workers—the *Have Nots*—onto reservations. All so the billionaires and their cronies—the *Haves*—could enjoy the remaining least polluted and scenic parts of the planet. Jake would probably never grasp just how much healthier and freer life was at Gentle Acres compared to existence inside a walled Workers' Zone filled with holographic distractions and drugs to keep the *Wanna-Haves* obedient and docile.

When they weren't working their twelve-hour shifts, slaving away to meet the needs of their Have-It-All masters, the Wanna-Haves received the appropriate schooling. They were brainwashed from infancy into believing they would become demi-gods themselves someday and possess great material wealth. There were few, if any, who realized the Haves would never allow it.

Did Jake feel he already had a foot in the door because of his job with the Agency? That he'd have the right someday to enter the world of the Haves? Or that eventually the luxury of being able to come and go freely throughout the Zones would be his, no matter his humble origins? In over twenty years of Authority rule, Zonta had never heard of such a success story. Too bad Jake would never believe her if she revealed the lie for what it was.

"I look good in this older style, don't I?" Jake's deep baritone voice jarred her from her thoughts.

Zonta turned from where she was slicing bread. The t-shirt and the drawstring pants weren't quite skintight, but they did reveal the musculature of his arms and legs and his nice ass. *Simple lines* were what Daphne called those body outlines once. Art was all about drawing simple lines.

"Yeah, the loose style works for everybody." Zonta smiled.

"You always wear tailored clothes with buttons and zippers and pockets and such?"

Jake shrugged. "They're the only clothes available for sale in the shops, so . . . I guess I do."

"You have to spend *money* to clothe yourself?" It had been so long since Zonta had even seen currency that the word *money* sounded foreign and dreadful coming from her lips.

"*Money makes the world go 'round,*" he replied, quoting an ancient adage venerated by the Haves.

"How sad." Zonta shook her head. "Too bad you don't have artists in the Workers' Zone to help you find your own style. The Haves hog all the designers and dressmakers for themselves, huh?"

Jake raised an eyebrow. "Designers? Dressmakers? I'm not even sure what those are, really."

She narrowed her eyes. "How old were you at the time of the Turn Over?"

"I was in middle school when we first moved to a Workers' Zone. But I wasn't paying too much attention to things, and the Turn Over just sort of *happened.* I just kept my head down, enjoying video games and trying my best not to get noticed by the Army. No way did my mother want her only child sent off to be killed in some heathen land. Luckily, the Authority did away with war."

No, you were given a gun and told to round up your fellow citizens into labor camps and told that didn't count as warfare. The Agency spotted you and decided you weren't half stupid and could be trained for domestic use, so they sucked you in instead. You never had a chance, did you? You missed out on learning how to think for yourself.

Zonta bit her lip as a thought struck her. *It's time someone helped you become truly independent. Then you'll talk, and we'll know what you know.*

Zonta retrieved the bowls and spoons, ladled some soup into each bowl, and placed them on the table. "Soup's on."

They ate in silence for much of the meal. Jake's eyes grew wide at his first taste of the soup. He couldn't seem to get enough.

"Slow down. You act as if you've never tasted anything in its natural state before. Your digestive track probably isn't used to whole foods." She patted his hand. "I don't want you to become sick like some who moved to Gentle Acres from the Zones did the first time they ate too much of our homegrown veggies."

"What?" Jake dropped his spoon into his bowl with a splash. "There are Zone workers actually living *here*?"

The incredulity on Jake's face was genuine. Zonta could tell he found the idea anyone would leave the Zones for more than a short break unheard of. No one could fake the doubt and confusion she saw in his eyes.

She smiled. "Finish eating, and I'll introduce you to some."

Despite her warning not to over-consume, Jake continued to wolf down the vegetable soup and spelt flour bread like it was going to be taken away from him any minute. He waited patiently as Zonta sipped her soup slowly and had another piece of buttered toast before rising from the table.

"All right. Let's go. You can help me wash the dishes when we return."

CHAPTER EIGHT

Zonta watched Jake grab his backpack from the corner of her eye, trying hard not to act as if he was anxious about its contents. She figured he must have several tracking and recording devices currently active that needed monitoring. Without giving him a head's up, she veered toward the front door, forcing him to zip the backpack shut to follow her outside.

"Ryan and Mac should be out on their driveway about now, chatting with folks and taking in new jobs." Zonta turned north on the sidewalk. "They live just a few blocks up."

He raised an eyebrow. "What kind of *jobs* do these gentlemen take in?"

"You'll see. Allow me to point out some interesting sights as we stroll. It's a lovely evening, don't you think?"

Before they could take a dozen steps, Jake stopped dead in his track, staring at the signage in Madison's yard next door.

"*The Madison Haywood Memorial Garden and Community Center, dedicated to our beloved dead and to the ultimate defeat of fascism and greed,*" he read aloud. "What does it mean?"

"Madi had a way with words." Zonta sighed. "I miss her so much. We all owe her so much. She and David talked about taking over the neglected acreage of the airport behind our neighborhood for several years before the Turn Over began. Together they planned an urban farm to feed everyone if the worst came to be—which, of course, it did."

"Didn't you join them in the planning? You seem to know

a lot about growing things."

"I helped out a little at the start, but I was taking graduate school coursework then. I was a young married woman, so my attention was focused elsewhere. I threw in my two cents now and then, and I've modified their plans as necessary over the years. Their ideas were sound, though."

Jake looked puzzled. "Still, those dedication words on the sign . . . You approve of it?"

Zonta nodded. "It's what Madi wanted it to say and what she wanted us to do with her home after she passed away, so it's what we did. Several of her charcoal sketches and David's detailed garden maps are framed and hanging in the front room. We use Madi's place for garden planning sessions. Her former bedrooms and home office have become a horticultural library and a shrine to her leadership. I can take you on a tour of the house if you like."

"Maybe later." Jake seemed to be scanning the street in front of them carefully, observing the other residents mingling outside for evening strolls and bike rides. "There seems to be a lot of activity here in the early evening hours."

Zonta snorted. "Yeah, I didn't tire everyone out today, forcing them to slave away weeding and watering, if that's what you're thinking."

"I didn't say you were a slave master, did I?" Jake sounded hurt. "But the people in this area have to eat, and they can't expect you and a handful of others to do all the farm work for them, right?"

"Oh, I guess I have to forgive you for not understanding how we operate. We have a roster and rotate shifts, so it's not that onerous. We have plenty of help. Everyone pitches in."

"Everyone helps?"

"Those who aren't physically able because of health reasons help with food growing, gathering, and storing tasks in ways they can, so no one feels less than or that they're helpless. No one goes hungry here. No one feels worthless."

"No one?" He raised an eyebrow.

Zonta nodded. "No one. Ever."

They walked on in silence.

"Good evening, Zonta," Jefferson called out from his front stoop as they approached the corner. "Lovely weather for a stroll tonight, isn't it?"

"It most certainly is," she replied, waving. "See you later at the movie?"

"I think so." Jefferson nodded, giving Jake a quick, perfunctory glance. "I believe it's one of Danielle's picks."

Zonta smirked. "It should be very *educational* then, huh?"

Jake lowered his voice as they turned the corner. "Is that who I think it is? Jefferson Jackson, one of the leaders of *the* sit-in?"

"You mean the famous sit-in of religious and civic leaders who dared the Fat Man to arrest them all instead of kicking the poorer patients out of the hospitals and into the streets? Yes, that's the one."

"I was sure Jackson had been captured and recanted his part in the illegal protest after we . . . After the Authority took complete control of this region."

Zonta laughed and shook her head. "Some brainwashed newsreader-puppet told you a fairy tale, and you automatically believed it? You don't strike me as being that gullible, Jake."

"But I saw videos of his arrest." He frowned. "There was a big trial of the sit-in leaders, as I recall."

"I'm sure there was some great electronic doctoring of the raw videos to make it look like Jefferson had repented and changed his ways and learned to embrace Big Brother. But the truth speaks for itself. He's been my . . . uh, *neighbor* for many years."

Zonta smiled to herself.

"Why would anyone alter the facts about Jackson's arrest and trial? Why would anyone change any historical documentation about what happened back then?" Jake wondered aloud.

Zonta stopped, turned to Jake, and stared into his gray eyes for several moments. "You really don't know? Let me ask you a question. After Jefferson's so-called *conversion* to the cause of the benevolent dictator, did things calm down in the Zones?"

"Yes, it did. All men of the cloth support the charitable ways of the Authority and preach cooperation and peace."

"*Men*, right." Zonta chuckled and began walking. "No women or gay clergy allowed in that high circle, am I right?"

Jake shrugged. "*Those men who practice abominations and don't repent will be rehabilitated for their own good* is how the law goes. It's pretty much the standard practice in the Zones."

"Uh-huh. It explains why most of those who were persecuted because of their gender or sexual leanings fled and ended up here at Gentle Acres or one of our sister communities. But don't worry. Many of them have since reopened their churches. The Authority's prejudices didn't slow them down any."

Jake's mouth dropped open. "You mean, there are some of *them* here?" he whispered.

"Them? Oh, do you mean women?"

"You know who I mean." He crossed his arms. "The ones who commit abominations with little boys."

"From what I gather, you all got to keep the pedophile priests in the Zones. But if you mean LGBTQIA persons, then yes. We're going to talk to two of them right now."

Zonta strode up the driveway of a large, red brick ranch home. A tall, thin man in his late thirties was busy picking chili peppers from a raised bed. He turned and greeted them with a smile.

"Hi, Ryan! Is Mac about?" Zonta asked.

Ryan gave her a kiss on the cheek and sighed. "Oh, he's around here somewhere. He got a big pile of car parts in that last visit from the Scavengers, and he's bound and determined to build something worthwhile out of them. Let me flush him out for you."

Ryan strolled to the house and popped his head in the side door of the garage. "Oh, Mac, my dear, we have guests."

"Just a minute, my tall drink of water," Mac called out. "I've got myself all covered with oil or something worse that oozed out of this engine part. Amazing how great a shape it's in."

Ryan laughed and clapped his hands. "That's my baby for you — covered in grease and filth, but he still manages to look hot in those dirty overalls of his."

Zonta sensed Jake's growing uneasiness. He shifted his weight back and forth on the balls of his feet, acting as if he might make a run for it at any moment. The Authority had banned all public displays of homosexual behaviors in the Zones. Those who couldn't comply and hide their true natures were imprisoned. They were then put through a horrendously painful rehab program that supposedly cured them by transforming them into happy and functioning heterosexuals.

Ryan and Mac were two escaped individuals who proved how the Authority's *cure* was a total and complete failure.

"It's all right." Zonta placed a hand on Jake's shoulder to cease his rocking movement. "They're not contagious. They're our fellow human beings. And yes, they're a couple — a married couple. Jefferson performed the ceremony, as I recall."

"Darn right he did." Ryan held his head high. "It'll be five years this November. The Authority knows what they can do with their bigotry and hatred. I hope the Fat Man chokes on it."

Mac, a broad-shouldered, white-whiskered individual, exited the garage at that moment and gave his husband a peck on the cheek.

"I . . . It's just that I've not met any persons like these *gentlemen* before," Jake admitted.

"That you know of." Zonta smiled. "Humans come in all sorts of packages. The Authority wants you to think that only heterosexuality is *normal* and everything else is an aberration, but what do we know? Even Jefferson preaches that if Ryan and Mac are the way they are, then God made them that way for a purpose."

"God made Ryan for the purpose of picking out my clothing when we dress up since I have terrible fashion sense." Mac placed an arm around his lover. "Now, what can I do for you, Zonta and . . ."

"Gunderson. Jake Gunderson." It sounded like Jake was grinding his teeth as he barked out his name.

Zonta frowned. She'd been going to ask for a tour of Mac's workshop, but now she had second thoughts. Jake might not be able to behave himself and perhaps feel tempted to *eliminate the abominations* as the Agency had been tasked to do within the Zones.

"We were just taking a walk," Zonta began, "and I wanted to show Jake how self-sufficient we are here at Gentle Acres. I also wanted him to know that we always welcome refugees from the Workers' Zones."

"You'd better believe it, honey!" Ryan laughed and dusted off his lavender-colored shirt with a flick of his hands. "Those who can't breathe under the artificial domes and live the plain vanilla life the Authority insists upon often wind up here or similar places."

"Appears so." Jake's expression seemed to be one of confusion, betrayal, and surprise all rolled into one.

"You know, I hear tell there's a thriving gay bar scene over

at the City Park Collective these days." Ryan laughed. "Fig-
ures we'd immigrate to a more family-friendly area, doesn't
it, Mac?"

"Well, I was ready to settle down, and then we found this
empty house to fix up, and these good folks welcomed us
with open arms. It was love at first sight." Mac took Ryan by
the hand and gave him a quick kiss.

"Do you believe in love at first sight, Jake?" Mac asked.

"I don't know." Jake turned and gazed deeply into Zonta's
eyes. "I didn't use to, but perhaps I do now."

"It's scary, but it can be magical at the same time," Mac said
softly. "I believe it's best not to fight it."

"Love will win out. It always does." Ryan pulled his husband closer. "Oh, dear! That smell! Whatever have you been
playing with, sweetie? Go wash up this instance!"

CHAPTER NINE

W hat do I see in this woman's eyes that makes her so special, so different from the rest?

Jake realized at that moment that he'd fallen down the rabbit hole—an expression with a meaning he'd never been sure of until just then. Had he forgotten his mission, his duty to the Agency? No, he hadn't. But somehow his priorities had shifted in the last few hours—of that much he was certain.

Could I convince Zonta to come back with me to the Zone? Why would she ever want to live there? This place is as much a part of her as her dark eyes and full lips. She's like one of her grapevines in the garden . . . Her roots belong here. They draw sustenance here. It's here and only here where she can live and grow.

Zonta guided him away from the gay men's house to what she called a *gathering*. They were showing a movie there tonight, a video recording they'd dug up from some dilapidated building in the long destroyed downtown area of the dead city. She explained everyone loved to gather to watch movies in the best air-conditioned place in Gentle Acres, especially when the broiling heat of the sun beat down upon them as it set in the west.

"The Scavengers have been quite successful at digging stuff out from under all the rubble heaped on top of the Main Library," Zonta explained as they strolled down a long street. "The vaults in the library's basement storage areas were left intact. The Authority thought they could burn our books and blank out our minds, but it didn't work."

She stopped in front of what looked like an old-style

church with a half-toppled steeple and boarded up stained glass windows on the ground floor. Its sign announced it was the *Gentle Acres Community Center and Gathering Place*. However, in the background, Jake could barely make out the faint outline of a cross and the name *St. Paul's*.

The heathen regularly desecrate church buildings his mother had taught Jake from a young age. To him, it appeared as though they'd actually given the old church a new purpose and a new lease on life. What would be better for the community — a dead church or a living community center?

"Folks like Ryan and Mac have been a big help." Zonta took his arm and led him up the sidewalk to the main entrance. "They've rebuilt and maintained machinery and equipment that has allowed us to reconstruct our destroyed infrastructure. We've recreated our libraries and have maintained and stored as much as we can of the digital information that was previously available on the internet."

At the sound of the forbidden word *internet*, Jake's heads-up display leapt to life.

FIELD REPORT OVERDUE flashed in red repeatedly before his eyes, almost causing him to trip. Fortunately, Zonta's grip on his arm steadied him. She guided him into a crowded, darkened meeting room with a large screen suspended from the rafters.

They took a seat in a long pew toward the back of the former church sanctuary. A teenage girl with a large box suspended on two shoulder straps offered them a bag of what she called *popcorn*. Zonta took two bags, and they settled in with to watch what appeared to be a very old animation. It was so old that the characters seemed to have been hand-drawn and colored.

"I've always liked Daffy Duck." Zonta grinned and passed him a bag. "He's much funnier than white boy Donald Duck."

"I wouldn't know." Jake had a dim memory of watching

something called *Disney* when he was little. But those memories had been pretty much wiped out by time and the stress of living and working under the aegis of the Authority. "Is this stuff we're eating really corn? It tastes . . . different."

She laughed. "Yes, it's made from actual corn kernels. From what I hear, they give you something made from reconstituted corn fiber and genetically modified soy in the Zones. It's not quite the same."

Jake munched on the addictive substance and focused his gaze toward the screen. *FIELD REPORT OVERDUE. DETAILED EXPLANATION MANDATORY* flashed in front of his eyes, shouting at him in big red letters. There was no use putting it off any longer. He took a deep breath and began mentally typing to his superiors.

Scanner indicates no DNA residue from lost Agents in the vicinity. Currently building rapport with the community. Will continue to investigate and follow up on possible suspects.

The report was short but accurate. The scanner hadn't made as much as a *bleep* since Jake had arrived, and he knew from experience how sensitive the device could be. The latest model of DNA detectors could pick up a fingerprint or a microscopic fragment of hair or skin from a meter away. His scouting of the garden areas had been very thorough.

Jake had expanded the area the device could scan for slightly larger DNA samples to several meters as he and Zonta strolled through the neighborhood. If Agents Smith and Davis had visited this place, they had disappeared without leaving a trace, an almost impossible feat.

So why did their last check-ins indicate they were at Gentle Acres? Jake frowned.

"You're not laughing," Zonta whispered, then narrowed her eyes when she looked at him. "What's up?"

Jake slumped in his seat, meeting her gaze at her level. "Sorry. I don't see what's so funny about an anthropomorphic duck hitting another cartoon character with a hammer."

"You don't? That other character is Hitler. This is a classic piece of antifascist propaganda from the nineteen-forties."

Jake furrowed his brow. "The *antifascists* were the bad guys, or so I was taught."

Zonta stared at him. "Where did you go to school? I mean, before the big Turn Over?"

"I was homeschooled by my mother. She didn't want me to learn anything from *the impure, sick, and twisted demonic liberal teachers.* Or so she said."

"Oookay. Explains a lot."

The video ended, and the audience applauded. The dimmed lights came up, and someone announced there would be a five-minute intermission.

Jake wanted Zonta to know not everyone who had ultimately sided with the Authority and entered the Zones was violent or oppressive.

"It wasn't as horrible as you might think," he tried to explain.

She crossed her arms. "It wasn't?"

Jake tried to respond but found himself speechless. A lot of what he'd been taught had been quite horrible, very negative, and ultimately useless. He was fortunate that other influences outside his immediate family and the Agency had mitigated the worse of his training.

"You really were perfect fodder for the Agency, weren't you?" Zonta murmured several moments later. "You truly believed in the righteousness of the cause and that anyone who doesn't think exactly as you do deserves to be bombed, shot, or gassed out of existence."

She leaned closer and gazed deep into his eyes. "But after today, do you still feel that way?"

Jake didn't know what to feel anymore. He'd been briefed to act friendly to the natives as a method to gain their trust. The Agency wasn't always antagonistic toward those who had refused the safety and shelter of the Workers' Zones. They mostly tolerated and left the remnant of their former failed society alone, a testimony to its inherent weakness and foolishness in not following the Authority.

But Zonta had shown him that the people here at Gentle Acres weren't weak, and they certainly weren't foolish. They were organized and practical. They cooperated for the common good, which was more than workers did in the Zones. They cared and provided for all their members as well as strangers.

Jake froze. There was no way these peace-lovers could have killed the missing agents. It wasn't in them. They were content with simple things such as growing food and watching one-hundred-year-old videos. There was no way these people were murderers. The Agency had it all wrong.

And if the Agency had Gentle Acres and its inhabitants all wrong, what else might they be wrong about?

"I'm starting to see things from your point of view," he conceded. "It's . . . it's difficult to think that I might not have had all my facts straight. But I trust you, Miss Trustworthy. I do."

Zonta smiled. "Change can be scary, but it's a good kind of scary."

"Will you help me learn what all I've been missing? I'd like to know more." It was the first request he'd made for himself all day.

She pulled him toward her and kissed him passionately, then nestled herself in his arms. "Hmm, after the main feature, I'll give you another lesson if you like."

After the movie, Jake felt more confused than ever.

Zonta and the others seemed to enjoy the century-plus old film. They even stood and applauded the last scene where the little barber stood and valiantly gave a speech about *freedom and decency.* Jake thought he'd recognized the actor from other videos or photographs he'd seen, but the man had had a funny hat and cane as well as a little mustache in those visuals.

As the crowd poured out of the building into the dark and humid night, a tall, thin young woman wearing heavy red lipstick approached them on the sidewalk.

"Ooh, Zonta. Would you like to introduce your new friend to us?" the woman asked.

Zonta raised an eyebrow. "Oh, hello, *Danielle*. I haven't seen you for simply ages. How's it going?"

"I've been *bound* up for a while, but Daphne tells me it's okay to let it all hang out from time to time and be my authentic self." She tossed her straggly, shoulder-length brown hair over her shoulders. "Who's your handsome friend? I don't recognize the face, and I know everyone in these parts."

Danielle took a step closer to Jake and scanned him from head to foot. "And I mean *everyone*."

"This is Jake," Zonta replied with a matter-of-fact tone. "He's visiting from the Workers' Zone."

Danielle planted her hands on her bony hips and rolled her slightly bloodshot eyes. "So, Jake from the Workers' Zone, what brings you to these parts? Our fresh air? Clean water?"

Jake looked at Zonta for a way out of the conversation, but she simply smiled at him. He cleared his throat. "I'm learning more about Gentle Acres and its inhabitants."

There. It wasn't a lie, and it didn't reveal that he was on a mission to search for two missing agents.

"So, Zonta's giving you the tour? What have you kids seen so far? The farm? The library? The school?" Danielle shifted her weight from side to side. "The petting zoo?"

"Petting zoo?" Jake turned to Zonta. "You have a *zoo*?"

"She means our livestock barn," Zonta said through gritted teeth. "I see Daphne motioning to you, Danielle. You girls go and enjoy yourselves. Have a good night."

"See y'all later." Danielle winked before flouncing off to join a large redhead woman chatting with a group on the steps of the former church.

"Shall we go back to my place?" Zonta smiled suggestively.

Jake chuckled. "I thought you'd never ask."

They walked on in silence for a block. Jake admired the electric generators switching on at most houses with their quiet efficiency. The Authority claimed solar power went against the good of the people since it didn't give miners and oilmen jobs. But the air seemed less hazy, less pungent at Gentle Acres than in the Workers' Zones powered by natural gas and the remnants of coal-burning plants. Rumor had it that the Haves utilized solar and wind energies exclusively in their private compounds to the north in places located far from the intense heat and unpredictable weather of former temperate regions.

How kind of our exalted leaders to allow the workers to have efficient fossil fuel plants! Words the state propagandists cheered. Who were they kidding? The Haves knew exactly what they were doing, and they didn't give a damn about the fetid air quality or the frequent power brown-outs in the Zones.

"You okay?" Zonta asked, breaking the silence. "Was it the movie or Danielle?"

Jake sighed. "Both. Something is definitely wrong with your friend."

Zonta glanced at him askance. "In what way?"

"I don't know." He shrugged. "She just seems . . . *off* somehow."

"How?"

"Like she's hiding something important, or she is putting on a show."

"How is Danielle putting on a show?"

Jake wasn't sure what he meant. Maybe the clean air and

abundance of oxygen were getting to him. Could this be what happened to the missing agents? He stopped and took in another deep inhalation of the pure oxygen.

It felt good.

"I mean, why all the cosmetics?" he rambled on. "She had on more lipstick and eye color than even the leaders' wives and concubines wear for state occasions."

"Believe it or not, we do occasionally get supplies of cosmetics found by the Scavengers, but lots of us have experimented with making our own. Daphne — Danielle's partner — has mixed up some really wonderful colors for eye shadows and lip tint."

"You don't wear any, I notice."

Zonta shrugged. "I tend to sweat off make-up working outside most of the day. Why, do you think I need some face paint?"

Jake shook his head. "No, you're beautiful without it."

Zonta smiled. "Thanks." They started strolling again. "My ancestors wore face paint proudly — particularly when they were preparing to go to war against the white man."

"I should be grateful you haven't scalped me yet. Is that what you're saying?" Jake joked.

The icy glare that met his remark caused him to instantly regret his choice of words.

"Sorry." He cleared his throat. "You know, we have some Indians living in the Workers' Zones. They've done quite well for themselves."

"Reservations are nothing new to us, but the final slaughter of the buffalo and appropriating the remainder of our ancestral lands in the cooler latitudes by the Authority broke the spirit of many. I was lucky to be living in the city at the start of the Turn Over. I'm not sure I could have taken it if I'd seen the violation of our homes firsthand." Zonta shuddered. "The stories of those who fled in the last days that I've heard . . . I can't even speak them out loud."

Jake put an arm around her shoulders and was grateful she didn't push him away.

The starlight had broken through the red glow of the setting sun by the time they reached Zonta's doorstep. She opened the unlocked door and motioned him inside. She pulled him over to her sofa, and they were soon wrapped in each other's arms, kissing, stroking, loving.

"Isn't this what we were supposed to do at the movies?" Jake said, coming up for air.

Zonta laughed. "I wanted you to see the film."

"You mean, you wanted to educate me, not simply make out in public."

She averted her eyes. "Well, there were children about. We adults have to set a good example for them."

"I wouldn't know. No adult ever set a good example for me." He sighed. "And where do all these children come from exactly?"

Zonta gasped. "You mean you don't know?"

"Of course, I understand basic biology, it's just that . . . There are so many kids here and so few in the Zones. Many don't make it past their first or second birthday."

"That is so sad. The pollutants and the radioactivity tend to take their toll on the youngest and the oldest." She sat up straighter and leveled her gaze at him. "Tell me something. What's the average lifespan for a worker? And don't tell me what you're told by the Authority — tell me what you've observed in your own zone."

Jake crumpled up his face in thought. "I'm going to guess and say about sixty? Sixty-five years?"

"Wow, only sixty-five? You've met Jefferson. How old do you think he is?"

"If he's the man in the videos I'd seen from before the Turn Over, then . . ." Jake did the math in his head. "Nah, he can't be that old."

Zonta nodded. "He is. We had a big seventy-fifth celebration for Jefferson last year. And he's not the oldest in Gentle Acres by far."

Jake laughed. "The next thing you'll tell me is that you're older than me."

"I probably am. How old were you when the Fat Man took over as the Authority? I was in college."

"I was a teenager. Close enough." He touched the silver growing at his temples. "We just age faster in the Zones."

She reached out and stroked his hair, then pressed her lips to his forehead. "You wouldn't have to if you stayed here."

"Stayed here?"

Jake couldn't picture himself ever letting Zonta go. But he also couldn't imagine himself living in a society where people felt they didn't need to lock themselves away from their neighbors. Could he live in a place where people felt comfortable sharing their food and possessions because they were confident others would return the favors someday? It was alien. *Unnatural* was the word he'd been taught by his mother and the Authority. All human beings had the instinct to fight those unlike themselves and take what they needed, no apologies, no questions asked.

A dog eats dog world where only the strong survive. Could I endure if I became as gentle as Zonta and the others here?

A burning sensation at the side of his neck ripped Jake's thoughts and body away from the woman he had come to love in one short day. He stood and staggered away from her, blinded by the intensity of sensation.

"What is it?" Zonta's eyes flashed concern. "Are you in pain?"

Jake nodded and gasped as a wave of searing pulses engulfed his entire body. "I'm . . . I'm being punished. Guess they've been reading my bio-signs all along. They can tell how much I'm attracted to you and what all we've been up to."

Zonta rushed to his side as another excruciating series of impulses wracked him. He dropped to his knees.

"The bastards!" Jake cried out. "They swore they'd never eavesdrop on my activities as long as I got the job done. Should have known they'd lie. Lying is second nature to them."

Zonta nodded. "Never trust those who see you only as a pawn in their games." She put an arm around Jake's middle and helped him to his feet.

He hobbled into the bedroom and lay down on the bed. He needed every ounce of energy he had to concentrate on fighting the internal attack.

"I'll go get help. It's okay. I'll be back soon," she promised.

"Thank you," Jake croaked before he lost consciousness.

Jake woke to Zonta arguing quietly with someone else in the room.

"It's not the same as before," she said. "We don't have to act the same way this time. I believe we stand a good chance of flipping him. Let's don't lose this opportunity."

He lay semi-conscious on Zonta's bed — at least he assumed he was still in the same place. His vision was blurry, and his head and spine ached terribly. He couldn't move a muscle to speak or tap a finger if he tried. Those neural implants were killers, literally and figuratively. The Agency could hit a button and send a lethal signal to his brain any time they deemed necessary for the good of the Authority.

That begged the question then — why wasn't he dead?

"Opportunity. Sure, there's always a chance, but how often has that proven to be the case in the past?" A deep male voice was speaking now. "We've got to protect our own."

Jefferson Jackson? Jake remembered the resonance of the once-notorious orator.

"Of course we do," Zonta agreed. "But Jake has skills and

knowledge we could use to protect us from what's coming."

"Ooh, Zonta's got it bad," a third, higher-pitched voice said. It was familiar and yet not. "I told her she could have fun but not to fall for her mark. But would she listen? Nope."

Has Zonta fallen for me? Fallen in love? There's hope I'll make it out of here alive if she has. If only . . . If only I hadn't fallen for her as well. I am vulnerable and might as well be in a body bag. The Agency will not be happy with me. There is no forgiveness for an agent gone native . . . an agent who has lost sight of his sole purpose of serving the Authority. I just pray the end will come swiftly.

CHAPTER TEN

"You've got it all wrong, Daniel. All wrong." Zonta stood taller and spoke with all the determination she could muster. "I only want what's best for Gentle Acres and the Movement. I'd never jeopardize either of them. Never."

She glanced down at Jake lying unconscious on the bed and swallowed back her tears. She couldn't afford to be seen acting soft for their guest. She had to pretend he didn't mean anything to her, for his sake as well as her own.

It had been difficult for her watching Daniel and their resident medic, Bernadette, extract the neural implant device inserted into Jake's neck. The blood loss, the chance of infection, the possible neurological damage . . . Any or all of these could kill or maim him. What sort of creatures would implant such a torture device into one of their servants?

Bernadette sat quietly at Jake's side, monitoring his vital signs and saying little. The petite blonde had mentioned earlier how they couldn't be certain if they'd removed the device in its entirety. She was fairly certain the wires that stretched out from the nexus into all parts of his body were still intact.

"It's probably next to impossible to extract the extensive network of microscopic cables from his central nervous system without killing him," Bernadette had said. "The Agency makes sure their soldiers never go AWOL. So much so they're willing to kill them first with a lethal pulse if they have the merest indication of them *going native*."

Had Jake been thinking of going native? Leaving the Workers' Zones for good? Zonta smiled to herself. *Could I have reached him after all? Perhaps he at least wants to stay with me a little while longer.*

"Well, now that he's officially offline with the Agency, we do have a bit of a breather," Daniel grumbled. He picked up an unsoiled towel and wiped the remainder of his lipstick off, then tossed it away. "After he's healed up here, I'll take him to the safe house."

"Have we rounded up all his tech?" Jefferson queried. "I don't want to spend sleepless nights combing over every dang inch of our turf looking for signal boosters and other tracking bits like last time. I'm just surprised he hadn't found anything yet and pegged us as accomplices."

"I kept him *busy,* really busy like you told me to." Zonta hoped she wasn't blushing unduly. "That was my mission, wasn't it? Keep him busy and out of your hair so the next steps could commence unheeded?"

Daniel nodded. "Yes, you did your job well. Sorry if I was curt with you earlier, Zonta. It's just the stress and now this . . . this *person* lying here will be my responsibility un-til . . . whenever." He began to pace the small room. "It probably would have been better to let the Agency explode his brain from within. Easier and far less messy for us."

Daniel paused and pursed his lips. "Hmm . . . You think the *petting zoo* might enjoy another late-night snack?"

"Enough!" Zonta rushed Daniel, pushing him out of the bedroom and toward the front door. "You forced our hands last time. Gentle Acres is not your slaughterhouse! These are human beings we're talking about—not chickens."

"Calm down, guys," Jefferson begged. He stepped in be-tween Zonta and Daniel and placed a hand on the door. "Let's not come to blows. We're peace-lovers, remember? It's bad enough we've had our losses fighting these fascists over the years. Let's not fight among ourselves."

Zonta allowed Jefferson to guide her and Daniel to the sofa before he sat in an armchair opposite. She was glad to have

Jefferson on her side — on the side of Gentle Acres. Sometimes the Movement operatives like Daniel were over-demanding. To survive in the post-Turn Over world, the communes and gardens, collectives, and co-ops needed intelligence and protection from the Authority. The Movement provided it. But the price they'd paid . . . Was it worth it?

Jefferson cleared his throat. "Okay, Daniel, what exactly are you going to do with our *guest* once he's recovered from his surgery?"

Daniel bit his slightly cranberry-tinted lower lip and hummed a moment. "Let me think about it. Standard operating procedure for our cell is to take all potential hostiles to a safe house away from the civilians. We're supposed to keep you all out of the fray, and I apologize that's not always been the case in recent times. But needs must."

"And after you get him to a safe house?" Jefferson queried. "What then?"

Zonta smiled at her former lover.

Jefferson grinned encouragement back.

Thank you for asking what I desperately wanted to know. I know I can count on you.

Daniel shrugged. "The safe house isn't really just one house. It's not even one place. It's just a drop-off and pick-up spot among cells in the Movement. A larger group of us will decide Agent Jake's ultimate fate. If he can be turned and we're confident of his loyalty, he'll probably be with us at the *celebration* we're planning in a few months."

"And if he can't be turned?" Jefferson stared hard at Daniel.

He would get a straight answer out of the young transexual. Zonta was certain of it.

"If he won't join me as Robin Hood and play along with my merry band of men, women, and others?" Daniel shifted his weight in his seat as if the words he spoke inflicted great discomfort. "Then you really don't want to know what will happen to him, do you?"

Zonta sucked in a breath, fighting back a sob.

Jefferson shook his head slowly. "No, that's fine. Just promise us that you won't bring back any *souvenirs* like last time, all right?"

Daniel pointed at the older gentleman and winked. "Gotcha. No souvenirs this time. I promise. He'll disappear like so many millions of others."

Zonta swallowed hard. *Jake will disappear like my David. Like Jefferson's wife and daughter. Like Madison's grandchildren. Like an entire generation lost to the greed and violence of madmen.*

"He's stirring," Bernadette announced from the hallway. "I've given him some more of the calming tea, so if you want to speak to him before it knocks him out cold again, act now."

Zonta reached over to squeeze Jefferson's hand in thanks and headed to the bedroom.

Her stomach lurched at the sight of him. Jake's complexion had taken on a sickly grayish tint, pale even for a white person. Zonta would have sworn he was a ghost. So much blood loss . . . The Agency didn't make removing their built-in snooping devices easy.

Perhaps *ghost* was the best description to give him. Jake had slipped into her life, almost invisible, spying on her home and her people. He was never meant to be an actual part of her existence. Substance-less, without form, a momentary dream on a summer's day only to fade away with the rising of a new sun.

"Zonta?" Jake whispered. "Are you there?"

She knelt and mopped his fevered brow with a cloth given to her by Bernadette. "Sh, don't expend the energy talking. You're fine now. That ticking bomb inside your head has been removed."

"It's gone?" He blinked and tried to focus on her face. "How?"

"Our medic has had some experience with removing these

devices. She got it out just in time. We detonated it in the middle of the meadow. Luckily, the goats were all tucked up for the night in the barn."

Jake tried to move, but his actions were fruitless. He was agitated but very weak. "I can't stay here. They'll come looking for me. If they think it didn't explode in my head, they'll come looking for me. And God knows what they'd do to you. I can't let that happen."

The fear and dread in his eyes . . . He wants to protect me. Zonta crawled into the bed beside her lover and cradled him in her arms, comforting him. "Don't worry. They won't find you. You'll be long gone from here."

He relaxed and sighed. "You'll be coming with me?"

She shook her head. "No, my work is here."

"But you'll be in danger. I can't leave you to face them alone." Jake tried to sit up but immediately collapsed. "Damn it! There's no way I'm leaving your side. These men are professional murderers."

"Harsh label." Zonta raised an eyebrow. "Aren't they your co-workers?"

Jake closed his eyes and grimaced. "Yes."

"You were trained to kill the Authority's enemies, too, were you not? There's no need to deny it, Jake. I understand."

Jake didn't reply. He pulled her closer instead.

"I'll take that as a yes." She kissed his fevered cheek. "Your Agency training could come in useful."

"Useful?" he croaked.

"Not so much at Gentle Acres, but useful to others that we come into contact with from time to time. We call them *Protectors.* Like the Scavengers, they interact along the edges of the Workers' Zones and elsewhere. They provide intelligence reports and help us maintain our autonomy from the Authority."

He frowned and took a shaky breath. The sleeping herbs

were starting to take effect. "You're saying that you . . . you want me to join . . . a rebel cell?"

Zonta stroked his head, softly sighing. "It's the only viable option at this point. You can't go back to the Agency without your implanted communications device because they'll ask too many questions that I don't think you can answer. They'll be forced to kill you. And we can't let you stay here because that'll only draw more agents to Gentle Acres and threaten our way of life. Your only choice is to cooperate with the Protectors."

"But I . . . want to stay . . . with *you*. Zonta, please don't send me away . . ."

Jake's eyes fluttered closed, his muscles relaxed, and he fell into a deep sleep. Zonta kissed him and then gently rolled him to his back, arranging the pillows to support his neck. She then stood at the foot of the bed and watched his breathing deepen for several minutes.

He had lost a lot of blood and would need several days of rest before he was strong enough to leave with Daniel and the others. While he was healing, she needed to do her best to convince him that joining Daniel's cell was not just necessary, it was imperative.

If he didn't go with the Protectors, how could she live with herself knowing she'd sent another lover to his death?

The last phone conversation Zonta had shared with David on that fateful day painfully unearthed itself from her memory.

"You're always saying how I need to take my studies seriously — yet you want me to take time out of my schedule to attend yet another demonstration? What purpose will it serve, David?"

"You're not listening to me, Zonta. We have them on the run. They're beginning to back off on their demands. We'll show them that the faculty and students are united against this restriction of our rights to privacy and the freedom to teach and study subjects of our own choosing."

"But they'll just shut us down like they did last month at State U. These assholes don't believe in a liberal arts education. They don't even believe in science! They just want robot workers and mindless foot soldiers. Most of my classes qualify under their new guidelines only because the fascists feel learning about growing food and restoring the soil is a necessity in their new world order. But give them time, and they'll figure out my Master's degree isn't about commercial agriculture. Then where will I be?"

"If our world falls apart, what good will your degree be? Please say you'll come down to the school tonight and march beside me, Zonta. Please?"

Zonta hadn't relented. She'd ended up pleading a headache and eyestrain and then hung up abruptly on her beloved husband, never to hear his voice again.

Never to see his face, to taste his lips, to touch his hands ever again.

Never to know what had become of her David and so many others as the bombs fell from drone planes like raindrops, silencing all opposition.

Within days, the entire city had ground to a halt. Within weeks, the country was no more, fractured into concentration camps and the newly titled *Zones* where the Haves and the Have Nots were separated for their mutual well-being, or so they were told.

How did they not know this was inevitable? How had David been so blithely unaware of the danger, so damn optimistic that with a few signs and chants the fascists would evaporate like fog on a sunny morning?

No one had been prepared for the devastation, or so it seemed in retrospect. Taken off guard, the survivors had huddled together. They'd done whatever it took to preserve some semblance of order in the insanity of the newly titled *Authority* and its incessant need to dictate the fates of the masses.

Zonta hadn't had the time to grieve her precious David. She and her neighbors had immediately begun saving seeds and preserving what food stocks they had or could acquire from the rubble of their city. They had banded together, helping reunite families and providing shelters in the houses and buildings that hadn't suffered significant damage in the quelling of rebellion.

Eventually, things had settled down and a new order of life emerged — one that was at times physically challenging and emotionally fraught with harrowing moments of post-traumatic stress. Zonta had endured by helping others to survive. She'd held onto hope above hope that her David would one day walk through the doors of the small bungalow they'd shared as man and wife for only a handful of years.

But by year five of the new world order, it became clear that those who had *disappeared* were gone for good, their final resting places never to be found. Most of Zonta's neighbors had adapted well and mourned their losses, and moved on. Together they had built Gentle Acres and the community surrounding it and looked forward, not back.

Horror stories from those who had been swept up into the Workers' Zones had leaked out from the first days of their formation, and refugees occasionally appeared on their doorsteps. They were usually welcomed with open arms. One such refugee had been Daniel.

Daniel, a trans-individual with a mission, an almost holy quest to see the bastards who'd destroyed his family and friends, city and country, suffer greatly for their sins.

This was the man she was supposed to entrust Jake's care and safety to without hesitation.

"Do you think he'll be ready to travel by daylight?" Daniel asked Bernadette in the hallway several minutes later.

Zonta turned an ear toward the bedroom door in order to eavesdrop.

"Give him a couple of days," Bernadette advised. "Without a transfusion it's much harder to heal when your body is forced to replace that much blood."

"We won't have the choice if the Agency comes looking for him. Or his body—they probably assume their *little lesson* killed him."

Bernadette whistled. "I'm highly impressed that it didn't. From what I've heard, these devices are ninety-five percent lethal once detonated, and the five percent who survive become total mental vegetables. We got to him just in time."

"You're sure he's not a squash? He looks a bit like a white eggplant." Daniel chuckled. "He's not much use to us unless he can hold his own weight and give us any intel he has on their operations in this area. If he's a zero upstairs, we might as well compost him and feed him to the pigs."

How dare you! Zonta spun around and confronted Daniel in the hallway. "Get out of my house! Leave Jake with me. I'll nurse him back to health. I promise you'll have your new cell member in a few days."

Daniel raised his hands and shook his head. "It's okay. I was just joking. I don't mind staying put with Daphne this week. I'll be nearby if trouble raises its head. You know where to find me."

Zonta pushed Daniel outside onto her front stoop. "Stay away until I say you can come back!"

Bernadette gathered her medkit. "I left some pads and gauze by the bed along with the calming tea. I'll check with our blood donors, too, just in case. Let me know if his fever spikes."

Zonta took a ragged breath. "I will. Thank you, Bernie. You are a life-saver."

Before Zonta could shut the door behind them, Jefferson rose from the sofa and took her into his arms.

"It'll be all right," he whispered, caressing her hair. "You'll see. We'll be all right once Agent Jake is better."

"Will we?" Zonta wondered now that Jake was most

decidedly ensconced in her life if she would ever be *all right* again.

"If he's what you want, we will be," Jefferson murmured. "I know Gentle Acres is your life, but I also know you need more than a vocation and communal activity. You need a special someone to love and care for."

She smiled and blinked back tears. "I have you, Jeff."

He chuckled. "Well, thank you, but I know for a fact you need someone closer to your own age. God willing, Jake is that man. He'll be there for you."

She pulled back and studied his expression. "Do you really think so?"

Jefferson shrugged. "He's beaten the odds thus far. Let's put our trust in the Almighty to pull him through."

Zonta snorted. "Put my trust in some mythical all-powerful being who pulled us through the Turn Over according to some? I'd rather place my trust in Bernie's surgical techniques."

"Then do that." He tenderly kissed her forehead and turned to leave. "Let me know if you need any help with the patient."

"I will."

Zonta saw Jefferson to the door and gently closed it behind him before returning to keep vigil by Jake's bedside. It was going to be a long night, but the flood of memories that continued to pour into her consciousness would keep her awake. Perhaps they might bring her some perspective to their current situation.

Perhaps they might even drive her a bit mad—but in a good way. To take the path she had chosen with Jake, she knew she would need all the energy and determination of a crazy woman to make it work.

CHAPTER ELEVEN

Jake sighed and turned over again, semi-conscious, remembering a dream that took him back home and into years past, long before he joined the Agency, before the Turn Over to the Authority. Back when his mother was young and without the worry lines that deeply etched the corner of her eyes for most of her existence.

Why was it in dreams everything seemed to glow with such brilliant colors? In this one, his mother wore a bright yellow dress, and she was uncharacteristically smiling. If there was a color to describe his stepfather, Clint, it would be black — or perhaps red with anger. Yeah, that was it. Vivid, crimson red.

Although he couldn't recall the details of the dream, the memories it invoked followed him into wakefulness.

His stepfather was angry most of the time. Angry and set on vengeance against some unknown force in the universe that never let him get ahead. He was always yelling about how one day he, too, would make the billions his idols made without breaking a sweat. He'd own the same kind of trophy wives and mansions to declare his success. He sure as hell wasn't a loser! He was *owed* a decent living.

Clint constantly berated Jake's mother for her failure to maintain an immaculate home and for saddling him with a rambunctious *spawn of Satan* — his loving nickname for Jake. Young Jake could do nothing but shiver in the corner, impotent to protect his mother from the psychological abuse and fear inspired by his overbearing stepfather.

Above all else, Clint worshipped what he called *self-made men*. Young Jake had wondered if these men had somehow created themselves from clay in the Garden of Eden—his mom's favorite Bible story. But his stepfather might as well have been made of clay, because in the end, he was easily broken.

Clint's attempts to get ahead in the Authority were thwarted repeatedly. According to him, he hadn't made the right connections or married into wealth early enough. Instead, he had settled for Jake's mother. She was a woman of good standing, willing to submit to her husband's will, like all women should, but one without a last name that could provide her spouse any power.

Get ahead or get out of my house was his stepfather's instruction when Jake hit his teens. So Jake worked hard to get ahead in the new order, but only by sheer dumb luck had he finally succeeded in gaining admittance into the Agency Academy. The son of one of the Haves had been killed in a drunk driving accident right before the start of school. Jake's entrance test score—being a dozen or more points higher than the dead kid's—finally convinced the regents to let him fill the empty slot. Jake could tell that they resented his lowly status.

Once at the academy, Jake knuckled down and studied hard, gaining a reputation as a fair and honest individual. The Haves could trust him not to screw things up. After a top ten placement in his class, a series of partners, and a promotion or two, he'd finally gained the right to handle cases alone. He was rewarded for his loyalty and work ethic with a fine home in the Wanna-Haves Zone, and his mother couldn't have been prouder.

Still, his stepfather never appreciated the strides Jake had made to put their family nearer to the top of their society. Nothing Jake did would be enough for the abusive old drunk.

Neither could Jake convince his mother to leave Clint. She had been indoctrinated to accept her horrid lot in life since long before the Authority took power.

Gradually Jake stopped trying to make others think well of him and his family. He started caring more about what was in it for him — what *he* wanted.

And at long last, he knew what he wanted — Zonta.

"Are you awake?"

Jake heard Zonta's voice as though he was still dreaming. He imagined her standing in front of him in a diaphanous dress, the sun reflecting off her ebony hair and casting a golden glow about her, her smile dazzling and inviting. She was beckoning him into her garden, into her home, into her arms, into her life . . .

But to be in Zonta's life, he would have to leave behind all he had worked for. The life he'd struggled desperately to achieve in the Workers' Zone in a vain attempt to impress his worthless stepfather, his anxious mother, and so many others.

"Looks like you need a few more minutes of shut-eye," Zonta pronounced with a sigh. "I'll check on you again in an hour."

Jake's eyes popped open. "Wait," he croaked. "You're here?"

Zonta sat beside him on the bed and touched his forehead. "Good. The fever's passed. You think you're able to swallow some soup?"

Jake tried to speak but ended up merely grunting an affirmative.

Zonta rose and returned momentarily with a mug of hot liquid. She sat and helped him raise his head enough to sip the vegetable broth.

After several gulps, he felt ready to call it a day. "I'm . . . so weak. Sorry to be a burden."

She smiled down at him, cradling his head in her lap. "No need to apologize. You survived something not many have. So I've been told. You're untagged. Free of your bug. You're like the rest of us now."

"I am?" Jake frowned. "No, they'll be after me. You can't mess with the Agency's tech and not get punished for it. Severely punished."

"That's what they tried to do—punish you—but we read the signs correctly and took swift action and saved you." Zonta shifted her weight uneasily and looked away. "It's good you're healing quickly, since you'll have to move on soon."

A shiver of cold dread swept over him. "Where will I be going? Will you be going with me?"

She shook her head. "I don't know the place, and I can't go with you. I have a farm to run here and people to feed. I'm not cut out for the type of life the Protectors lead."

"Protectors?"

"Our version of the Agency, only without all the high tech and the blessings of the Authority." Zonta forced a laugh. "They're always in need of recruits. They think you'd make one hell of a new member."

"Why would they recruit an Agent? I could turn on them. Why not just kill me? It's safer. It's what I'd do in this situation."

Jake blinked and tried hard to make out her expression in the dim light, but Zonta kept her face turned away. He raised an unsteady hand and caressed her cheek, wiping the tears from her high cheekbones.

"There, there. It's okay," he whispered. "I realize I'm in hostile territory. It's part of the job. I'm just glad to know you'll actually miss me when I'm gone."

Zonta took his hand from her face and squeezed it. "They won't kill you if you cooperate. *Please* cooperate with them."

He frowned. "What will I gain from cooperating with them?"

"You might find it's a better life for you here on the outside." She pressed his hand against her heart. "We don't rank you according to your last name or bank account. We respect you for who you are and how you can help the community. You can be your own person."

My own person? What does that mean? I've always been the person everyone else expected me to be.

A warm feeling enveloped him. "If I go along with these people willingly, would they let me come and visit you from time to time?"

"Possibly." She smiled. "Rest now and heal."

Jake's eyelids grew heavy. "Promise me when I wake up you'll be still here?"

"I'll be here."

The next few days were heaven on earth for Jake. Sure, he felt like shit and wondered if he'd ever regain his full strength again, but still . . . He had Zonta's full attention, and she had his. Boy, did she ever have his attention!

Zonta had passed her work chores on to her master gardener trainees. Jake enjoyed being waited on hand and foot by a beautiful woman by day, warmed by her voluptuous body at night. There was no need to impress the bosses. No need to look over his shoulder constantly for career backstabbers. He knew he should be wary, cautious, and less trusting of the situation he currently found himself in, but something deep inside him promised better.

Give Zonta's world a chance, his heart said. *Wait and see.*

By the third day of recovery, Jake's waiting was over.

"I see our patient is recuperating well." Daniel's accusing tone carried across the meadow. He approached them as Jake and Zonta strolled arm in arm through the livestock areas in the early morning sunshine.

Jake resented the interruption and frowned his irritation. This Daniel person always rubbed him wrong the way. Something was seriously amiss with the freak—and it wasn't because *he* was born a *she* as Jake had learned only recently. There was a certain *deadness* in Daniel's stare, a world-weariness that seemed incongruent for anyone of such a young age.

The children of Gentle Acres, on the other hand, shared none of this pessimism. As Jake observed them playing in the fields, they reflected only infinite vitality and joy. They laughed and joked with each other as they gathered berries or picked wildflowers. Zonta smiled and waved to them often, and they always smiled and waved back. They acted well-mannered and respectful of their elders. It was obvious the whole community cherished and cared for them. The children blossomed under the positive attention.

Jake wished he could have grown up in such a paradise.

Would I be a totally different person today if I had been raised here instead of in the Workers' Zone? Would I even recognize myself now if I had grown up here?

"You look like hell," the dour-faced Daniel pronounced as he reached Jake's side, looking him up and down. "Why did you drag this corpse out into the light? He'd be better off in a cave somewhere."

"I figured Jake could use some fresh air and exercise after being bedridden for so long," Zonta replied through gritted teeth.

Daniel snorted. "He didn't give you much exercise in bed is what you're saying, huh?"

Jake's fist ached to connect with Daniel's nose, but he didn't have the strength yet to take on anyone, including a pencil-thin freak. Zonta undoubtedly sensed Jake's agitation at the jibe. She placed a calming hand on his arm and guided him over to sit on a tree stump to rest and calm down.

"Can the attitude," Zonta commanded Daniel. "What do

you want?"

"You know what I want, my dear Zonta." Daniel sighed. "Well, it's not what *I* want so much, but what I must do for the sake of Gentle Acres and our children's future."

Zonta placed a protective arm around Jake's shoulders. "He's not ready to go yet. He's still healing."

Daniel shrugged and began pacing in a circle. "I know, I know, but I don't invent the rules. I just play by them. And we received intel early this morning that says the Agency is missing their man and wants to see a body."

"He's right. They'll want me dead or alive. They don't care for mysteries." Jake squeezed Zonta's hand as it rested on his shoulder. "I'm surprised they've waited this long."

Daniel nodded. "Things are a bit here and there back in the Zones, according to our sources, which explains the holdup. We're lucky for the delay, but it won't last forever. We figure they'll do as they did the last time, but this time they'll probably send at least a dozen agents at once to search Gentle Acres with a fine-tooth comb."

"A dozen agents?" Zonta's voice trembled. "You can't be serious."

"Deadly serious." Daniel stopped his pacing. "We can't afford to have them find dear Jake here without his dog tag in his head, either. Uh-uh."

"He's right. Agents caught without their tracker are usually executed on sight." Jake looked up into Zonta's eyes and grimaced as he saw the fear growing there. He swallowed hard. "It's best that I leave now. At least I'll have a head start on them."

"A head start is all fine and good, but they don't need to know how sophisticated we are." Daniel's blunt tone held no doubt. "We performed major surgery on old Jake's brain. They need to keep underestimating us and our abilities. It's better that way."

"The Agency *has* underestimated your strengths," Jake confirmed. "In their conceit, they believe you're a group of primitives surviving hand-to-mouth in the wastelands they left behind."

"Primitives—huh!" Zonta snorted. "Like they'd know the first thing about what being *civilized* means."

Jake nodded. "Yes, they don't understand how organized and structured you are. Or how you all communicate, trade, and connect with the other farms and communes in this area and elsewhere."

"See?" Daniel shook his head and finger. "It's like I've told you before, Zonta. We're just a bunch of backward yahoos. Nobody in the Zones takes us seriously. We're not seen as a threat to anyone, and we have no important allies . . . Well, none that the Authority knows of. And now that Jake here knows a lot more 'bout us than he should, it's time for him to pack his bags and go."

"To join the Protectors?" Zonta's voice sounded hopeful.

"Could be. But you know I'm not in charge of everyone." Daniel placed his hands on his hips and leaned forward. "Jake will have to make his own case for not becoming pig fodder."

"That's not funny." Zonta dropped Jake's hand and stepped toward the younger man, her face contorting with rage. "You promised he'd be located safe within your cell. You *promised*."

Jake stood and regained Zonta's hand so she wouldn't deck the asshole. "Is that how you got rid of the two agents who visited Gentle Acres before me? I haven't found a trace of DNA evidence they were ever really here. But if you fed them to the hogs . . ." Jake felt his stomach lurch. He stared Daniel straight in the eyes. "If you did such a despicable thing, I have orders to take you out now, without prejudice, and I'll do so."

"They were never here—at least not in life, that is," Daniel admitted, backing away. "They might have thought they were at Gentle Acres, but they'd followed their lead to our meeting place, which isn't all that far from here. That's where our cell confronted them."

"And you killed them?"

"If I told you it was an accident, would you believe me?" Daniel crossed his arms. "I supposed it was inevitable. They were very aggressive. They demanded answers that we weren't at liberty to share with them. We offered them the option of joining us and escaping the fascist hellhole of the Zones, but they pulled their weapons on us instead. They shot one of ours. One of our younger recruits, a nice young guy who was a good friend of Zonta's . . . So, yes, we were forced to protect ourselves. And yes, they were killed."

"Poor Ramon." Zonta's eyes misted. She pulled her hand from Jake's. "He always loved helping out in the gardens. I told him he was too kind and trusting to join the Protectors, but that's what he said he felt called to do—and he did."

She walked away, obviously needing time to be alone with her thoughts.

Jake grimaced. He should have realized the two agents had done something rash and stupid and gotten themselves killed in a shoot-out where they were outnumbered. It didn't help relations between the peoples of the Zones and the wastelands to shoot a kid, either. No subtlety there.

If there were two things the ever-increasingly corrupt Authority needed at this point, they were friends and good publicity. Holding the far-flung Workers' Zones together in some semblance of unity was a difficult balancing act for the Authority. Jake knew the Agency was expected to keep up their end of the bargain.

"You disposed of their bodies in the pigsty?" Jake asked, hating to hear the answer but knowing he must.

Daniel pointed over at the animal pens just beyond them.

"Yeah, these fat porkers will eat anything — and I do mean *anything* that was once alive. The clothing, personal effects, and what-not we gave to the goats. The tech we dismantled and spread about in neighboring areas, to be used in more worthwhile ways. Nothing is ever wasted here at Gentle Acres. The pigs eventually become bacon and hams. The goats give us milk and cheese."

Jake felt queasy and understood now why Zonta ate a strict vegetarian diet. He sighed. "So, if I cooperate with you and meet with your cell, I won't become this coming holiday's main course?"

"Yep, it's that simple," Daniel replied. "But we need to leave today — tonight at the very latest. We have a surprise — I mean an *operation* to plan."

Jake nodded. "Okay, but I'm not quite at my best. It might be a few days until I'm strong enough to keep up with you."

"No worries. We have transportation. And we won't put you through *basic training* right away." Daniel smirked. "You'll need a little remedial education first."

Here Zonta has been re-educating me with stories of how Gentle Acres and the other communal farms work together and thrive. What sort of lessons will I learn from the likes of this freak and his trigger-happy colleagues? How to hate and fear the Authority? It's too late — I already do.

"There's one thing I'd like to know before I leave Gentle Acres with you, Daniel," Jake began slowly. "Why this . . . this *disguise* you wear? Why do you act so miserable all the time? Is it the lot of a Protector — the misery and bizarre clothing choices?"

Daniel exploded in laughter. "Oh, you are special, Jake. You afraid I'll make you wear a dress?"

"Well, no, but . . ."

"I take it Zonta informed you I'm trans? You've never encountered anyone quite like me before, huh?" The hilarity faded, and Daniel lowered his voice. "I'm not wearing a *disguise* as you call it. I just feel better about myself when I dress the way I see myself, not in the way people in the Zones by law would force me to dress."

Jake frowned. "You believe you were born to be male and not female?"

"Wrong. I *know* I am a male and not a female." Daniel took a step closer with a somber demeanor. "The reason I seem miserable to you is that it's been a tough life for me as a trans person. Before the Turn Over, I would have had the opportunity for surgery to become the person I know that I am. My mind and body would match perfectly. But since we're forced to live in somewhat medieval medical times out here away from the rich farts in the Have Zones, I don't get that option unless . . ."

"Unless?"

"Unless we can overthrow the Authority and bring some friggin' democracy and compassion to everyone in this world. Including us *freaks*."

"Hey, I never called you that," Jake protested.

"I can read it in your face. I can hear it in your tone." Daniel leaned in until their eyes were within inches of each other. "Don't tell me you haven't suffered inside the Have Not Zones, Jake. No one gets a day pass from the Zones unless they've kissed ass for as long as they can remember. You don't get to call your own shots there. They've all been called for you since the moment you became their slave, right?"

Jake nodded. "It's funny how you all seem to know more about our lives in the Workers' Zones than we do about your lives here on the outside."

"Not so funny, really." Daniel pulled back and looked off into the distance. "I lived in a Workers' Zone until I was twelve. I ran away because I couldn't stand the torment anymore. I left and stumbled into Gentle Acres and never looked back. It's why I'm fighting for it to continue, unmolested by the Authority's narrow-minded viciousness. It's why I'm willing to give up my life for the chance that someday trans people like me both inside and outside of the Zones can once again have access to the surgery and care they need to feel whole."

Daniel stood taller and sighed. "It's a worthy cause to fight for, don't you think?"

"I . . . I understand." Jake spied Zonta approaching, her arms outstretched. "I think I finally understand how important it is to feel like myself, to feel *whole*. I will leave with you later tonight, Daniel, if you'll allow me to say my goodbyes before we go?"

Daniel smiled. "Hey, I get it. I need to say my *goodbyes* to Daphne, too. I'll leave you two alone until it's time."

"Did you get a reprieve?" Zonta raised an eyebrow as he pulled her into his arms.

Jake relaxed as he cradled her against his chest. "We have today until the sun sets. Whatever can we do in just one day?"

"I'm sure we can think of something," she whispered before their lips met and joined in blissful union.

Chapter Twelve

One month later

*W*ill I ever have a lover like Jake again? Will I ever want another man in this lifetime?

Zonta rested her head in the crook of her arm and dosed lightly under the apple tree where she and Jake had first made love. The ground felt soft and warm beneath her in the late afternoon sun, the grasses tender and cooler to her touch. Memories of his caresses, memories of his kisses aroused her. When had she learned to be so lavish in her affections to a stranger? To a man who represented a worldview as alien to her as hers was to him?

She sighed. If she had known how difficult it would be to let Jake go, would she have relented to Daniel's insistence that he leave at all? In the end, she knew she would. She could never risk the safety of her neighbors at Gentle Acres.

Zonta had often sat under the trees of the orchard and contemplated where she wanted her mortal remains to be buried. Somewhere in the gardens of Gentle Acres, she'd assumed, enriching the soil, but she had never picked out the exact spot before now.

This was the spot. She was certain of it.

Oh, David . . . I can never lie beside you. No one knows where your body lies, but in my heart, I know you are here. Here, in this orchard that we started long ago with Madison next door. I remember how we all loved sneaking out at night to clear the weeds and plant these trees. Who knew that our screwed-up world that shut down the airstrip would allow our little trees to grow into big ones?

Zonta rolled to her back and opened her eyes halfway, admiring the canopy of leaves above. *Do you mind that I have had lovers since you disappeared, David? I know you had a few girl-friends before we married, but I was never jealous of your past. I suppose you'd want me to be happy, to move on with my life, but how could I . . . How could I have moved on* then *when I didn't know where I was moving* to?

Zonta startled awake fully. Did she know now where she was moving to? Was she moving toward Jake and a better world he'd help create along with the other Protectors? Was she actually *living* now — no longer simply *surviving*? Was she no longer helping her neighbors survive day to day with no real hope they'd ever enjoy a brighter future?

Did she believe her future included Jake? Because with the operation plans Daniel had disclosed to her and Jefferson, the chance that Jake and the others would have any future at all was in extreme doubt.

No, she wouldn't think the worse . . . She *couldn't* think the worse.

Too long idle, Zonta sat up and stretched her arms over her head. Out of the corner of her eye, she spied a flash of metal in the grass near the base of the tree. Strange that she or anyone else hadn't spotted the pencil-sized piece of tech before now. She twisted and tugged at it, managing to free it from the ground where it was wedged.

She examined it closely and was fairly certain Jake had left it there, probably a beacon device of some kind . . . or a signal booster. With Jake's tech long gone with Daniel and the others, the device couldn't provide much of a threat to Gentle Acres' safety.

Or could it?

"Zonta!" Jenna called out a moment later. "Sorry to cut into your downtime, but it looks like we've got company."

Zonta stood and pocketed the small device in her work pail

alongside her trowel and secateurs. The faint sound of a small aircraft overhead made her heart race. Jake had arrived in a similar transport. She knew it wasn't him, it couldn't be him, but somehow she still felt happy. She headed toward her office and found a half dozen others milling about the barnyard, frowning and pointing up at their uninvited guests.

"It's doesn't appear to be landing, just circling. It's most likely routine patrolling," Jenna noted.

"Aren't we the lucky ones?" Zonta chuckled. "If they've not sent any agents in person these past few weeks to check on Jake's status, we're probably in the clear."

"You've got to wonder why they've not sent anyone before now." Jenna wrinkled her freckled nose. "It's not like Jake could tell the Agency he'd eliminated us from their list of suspects before he left with the Protectors. He couldn't communicate with his slave owners once Bernadette freed him of his brain chip, could he?"

Zonta bit her lip. "No, I don't think so, and Jake wouldn't communicate with the Agency because they think he's dead. But even if they think he's alive, they might have some kind of understanding that if they hadn't heard from Jake within a certain period of time, they'd come looking for him."

"So, we're not out of the woods yet." Jenna sighed and picked up her shears. "Well, the Authority knows where they can shove it on this beautiful sunshiny day. I'll be tending our berry patch if anyone from the Evil Empire comes knocking. Let me know if you need any help."

"Thanks, Jenna. I know I can always count on you."

Jenna tilted her head and observed Zonta closely. "It's going to be all right. You'll see Jake again someday. I know you will."

Zonta smiled wryly. "You are a treasure, but how can you be sure?"

Jenna shrugged. "Don't know. I just am."

Zonta hugged her friend and motioned for the others to get back to what they were doing before the distraction came along. Then she headed for her office. The device might have been activated when she pulled it free from the soil, and she didn't want to take any chances. She placed it in the bottom right drawer of her metal desk and returned to the barnyard area to raise the signal.

The grinning scarecrow on a stick seemed incongruent standing in front of the hanger-barn, but the decoration had proven its worth. Gentle Acres remained safe. Its inhabitants were none the wiser to the more distressing machinations that Daniel and the Protectors dealt with on a daily basis to keep them *free from fascist tyranny* as he liked to say.

Zonta looked off toward the horizon. Could it be this time, with Jake's help, it could spell the end of the Authority's threat to their existence?

It was long after dark before the signal was answered.

"Sorry to keep you waiting." Daniel leaned a shoulder against the office door. "It's been a busy day."

Zonta lifted her head from the book on sustainable agriculture she had been reading at her desk. "I didn't expect you — or your other self, rather, to show up. I'd thought you'd be far away from Gentle Acres by now."

"We went far away, but now we're back." Daniel plopped into the chair opposite and put up his feet, quickly folding his long skirt between his legs. "The local Protectors didn't really know where I was today. I went *undercover*, as it were."

"I see." Zonta felt her breathing quicken, her excitement rising. "By *we* you mean Jake? Is he with you?"

Daniel shook his head, unruly curls toppling into his face. "No, I'm sorry. He isn't with us."

Zonta fought back a gasp and screwed her eyes shut. "He's . . . somewhere else?"

"No worries, sweetie." Daniel lowered his feet from the edge of the desk, reached over to take Zonta's hand, and squeezed it. "He's very much alive and back at the Agency."

"The Agency?"

A sudden pain stabbed Zonta's heart. *Betrayal? No, there has to be another explanation, a better explanation.*

She cleared her throat. "Did he escape? Is he a mole?"

Daniel grinned. "All of the above. Sorry, I can't elaborate further. What I can say is that we're so close to our operation being a complete success that I can taste it."

Daniel chuckled. "I can taste it," he repeated, "and boy is it ever sweet."

Zonta heaved a sigh of relief. Jake was alive. He hadn't betrayed them. Still, he was in extreme danger if he had returned to the Agency. What if they discovered he had cooperated with those on the outside?

"How is Jake going to get out of the Workers' Zone after the operation is over?" She didn't want to hear the gory details if there wasn't going to be a happy ending, but she had to know.

"Honestly? I'm not certain, but he seemed confident he would be able to get out after . . . Well, whenever things settle down. If he's still alive, he said he will get out. And I believed him."

Daniel leaned forward and spoke in a confidential tone. "Jake is *very* motivated to return to Gentle Acres, Zonta. He's *very* motivated to see you again. He's going to return. I thought you'd like to know that bit of information."

"Thank you." She blinked back the tears forming in the corner of her eyes. "I needed to hear that."

"I know. Now, why did you signal us?"

Zonta reached into the bottom right drawer and retrieved the pencil-sized device. Daniel took it from her and twirled it around haphazardly.

"Hmm, this thing could explain why I heard the air patrol

overhead while I was hiking back into this area. Or not."

Daniel flipped the device up into the air, caught it, and then shoved it into a pocket in his backpack. "I'm not sure the Agency loses too much sleep over one misplaced cheap-ass signal booster. They figure we wouldn't know what it was in the first place or what to do with it, so they'll probably write it off." He grinned. "But of course, we do. Thanks for the contribution to our growing warehouse of Have Zone goodies."

Zonta nodded. "You're welcome. But tell me something — are they surveilling us because Jake came to Gentle Acres to investigate and then returned home empty-handed?"

"Ah, but he didn't. He didn't return empty-handed. I came along with him for the ride." Daniel raised a hand to cut Zonta's next question off before she could open her mouth. "No, I didn't go back to the Zone and then escape again. They're not tracking me down as far as I know. And I don't believe they're patrolling this area because of two missing low-level agents anymore."

Zonta raised an eyebrow. "No?"

"Uh-uh. It's got something more to do with what we've been planning for some time, which is why Jake had to go back into the Workers' Zone. We need inside intel, and he agreed, but he did so reluctantly."

Jake enjoys being free? He wants to live outside the Zones? With me?

Daniel's continued rambling interrupted Zonta's daydream. "It's not so much that he's convinced of the righteousness of our cause. Or the righteousness of the assholes in the Authority, for that matter, but because he knows . . . Well, he knows the risk he's taking by working for our side and that it's better if we win this hand. Far better."

"So, he's definitely on our side?" Zonta smiled. "Glad to know I was such a positive influence."

"I said he's *working* for our side, not *on* our side. I think Jake is ultimately on Jake's side, which is to be expected of anyone raised from an early age in that hellhole of capitalistic exploi-tation." Daniel rose. "If that's all, then I'm going to check in with Daphne."

"You do that. She misses you, you know?"

"She does. After tonight, I'm going to disappear for a while. You probably won't see me again. Ever. Not unless I'm lucky, and we haven't made any mistakes on our formula, or the Agency doesn't get wise to the plan before the . . ." Daniel made the sound of an explosion and mimed its fall out. "Fire-works."

Zonta nodded. "Sounds like we're going to have a proper celebration this summer."

Daniel placed a finger aside his nose and winked. "Re-member, you didn't hear it from me. I'm off now to get out of these horrible clothes, and Daph will be more than glad to help me."

Zonta smiled at Daniel's back as he sauntered away. If an-yone had nine lives and could go stealthily in and out of the Zones, always landing on their feet, it was her Daniel.

But did Jake possess cat-like abilities as well? Would he be able to retrieve the information he needed in the Zones and then come back to her? At times like these, Zonta wished she did believe in an all-knowing, omnipotent being to pray to for her lover's protection.

CHAPTER THIRTEEN

Homecomings are never all they're cracked up to be. So why should I expect this one to be any different? But it is.

Jake could count the number of times he had entered the Chief Agent's residence on one hand, minus three fingers. He'd been to the home of his supervisor's supervisor once before as an intern-lackey for his academy trainer. He had been honored with a nice shiny medal for ten uneventful years of service. He wished he'd been more observant all those years ago, but he'd been too worried about pleasing his superiors to note the layout of the monstrously palatial mansion.

Thinking back on it, his first visit to the Chief of the Agency's home was the first time he'd visited a private residence in the Haves Zone. The opulence, the chandeliers, the thick carpets ... Jake had thought he'd died and gone to heaven. Only heaven would look so clean and orderly and shiny and silken.

Even the wives of the Haves possessed an air of wealth and power about them in their fine-tailored gowns and dripping jewels. He'd been both fascinated and repulsed by them, especially when they looked down their noses at the poor boy who'd done good enough to gain admittance into their hallowed abodes for an evening.

"Agent Gunderson, you're looking well after your ordeal," the Chief Agent announced in front of his staff and a handful of sycophantic minor politicians. "The doctors said it's a miracle you didn't bleed out in the field. You are the first agent to experience such a dire reaction to a faulty comm chip."

"I was most fortunate I came upon a compassionate outsider who eventually brought me back here."

Jake fought hard to hide his smirk. The Chief knew full well that Jake's chip had been detonated purposefully by the Agency and not accidentally. The medics would have informed his superiors that the chances of him surviving such a detonation without professional help were slim to none since he had been far from a sterile hospital facility. That Jake had had the balls to show up alive at their doorstep and plead innocence in public wasn't something the Agency — or the Authority — knew how to deal with. Embarrassment with a hint of opportunity tinged their responses to him.

"Yes, most fortunate, and tonight the drinks are on me." The Chief laughed, and his entourage followed suit. The pack received their beverages from several passing waiters, then swaggered past Jake to join the higher-ups gathered in the ballroom.

Jake remained in the mansion's entrance hall, a room more than twice the size of the hovel he and his mother had shared after the death of his father. He scanned the crowd for the so-called *media darlings*. They played an important part in step two of Daniel's *big plan*, so there was no time to lose.

The sound of a woman pontificating on various subjects caught Jake's attention. Spying the loudest of the loudmouths in the corner, he made a beeline for her. The large-boned matron with masses of graying hair piled on top of her head resembled a statue of a Greek goddess Jake saw once outside a building in the Have Zone. The woman held court with the usual fanatics — media pundit wannabes and bored wealthy housewives who hung on her every word as if it came from the Almighty himself.

Jake inveigled himself a spot in the second tier of hangers-on and tried his best to look interested in what the old windbag had to say.

"Look who we have here!" she managed in between solil-oquies on the immorality of the workers daring to sleep to-gether without paying the lawful marriage tax. "It's our brave agent who escaped the jungles of the wastelands and lived to tell the tale."

Jake smiled and did his best to look humble as the women *ooh*ed and *ahh*ed, and the men slapped him on the back and gave him an envious look that said, *How is the action outside the Zones? Are those wild women all they're cracked up to be? They've gotta be better in the sack than the dumb and docile types we're stuck with here!*

"It wasn't as horrific as you might think," he began, trying his best to sound sincere and appropriately sympathetic to the Authority. "In fact, I think now is the time to welcome our lost brothers and sisters back into the fold. Our charity and gra-ciousness would be most appreciated by those lost souls."

An excited murmur enveloped the group. The media god-dess blinked and stared at him for a good thirty seconds be-fore finding her voice again.

"Why . . . this is the first I've heard of our glorious leader-ship wanting to extend our boundaries into the wastelands." Her beady eyes glowed with the excitement of landing an ex-clusive story. "Surely, the savages that dwell there couldn't begin to understand the nuances of our righteous life in the Zones and the blessings of law and order."

Jake smiled and nodded politely. He'd done it. She was hooked. "You'd be surprised. The natives are quite intelligent and amenable to training. They really are like lost sheep in need of a kind shepherd. It's time we learned more about them and teach them our ways."

"Really?" She leaned toward him and lowered her volume. "Would you like to come on my talk show tomorrow morning and tell my viewers more in an exclusive interview?"

"Are you sure?"

"Very sure!"

It worked. Daniel was right. The Haves are interested in reuniting with the friends and loved ones they left behind when they entered the Zones. We can force the Authority's hand by appealing to their ever-present need for goodwill among its leadership class. Once this talking head is done with me, they'll not hesitate to add a stop at Gentle Acres to the Fat Man's goodwill tour.

"I'd love to be on your show." Jake bowed graciously. "I can't wait."

The discussion ebbed and flowed around the media darling, her sycophants bubbling in anticipation of what all Jake might say on a live broadcast. There was no need to add to their increasingly creative scenarios. He slowly sipped his drink and allowed his focus to wander to happier thoughts.

Perhaps Zonta would be able to see him on the talk show back at Gentle Acres? Jake didn't doubt for a minute that they'd be able to rig up an antenna. What would she think about his performance?

It was the one thing Jake hadn't lied about to his superiors — that the natives weren't entirely clueless about the state of life in the Workers' Zones or the general mood of unrest. But in their arrogance, the Authority heads didn't concern themselves with how such knowledge could even remotely lead to their downfall. No, they were civilized men in the Zones. Primitives growing their own food via manual labor weren't seen as much of a threat or even a problem.

Since Jake had obviously survived the Agency's attempt to discipline him by blowing his head off, the two missing agents must have also survived after removing their communication devices and escaping into the wastelands. If Jake's tracking chip was faulty, then their tracking chips were also faulty. Jake's final report on the subject implied as much and that the two agents were more than likely to have gone rogue. His superiors had been convinced. The Agency would deal with them in time — if at all.

But for now, Jake's bosses had other more pressing matters

on their plates. *The Authority Goodwill Tour of the Zones* was in its final planning stages, and Jake was their newest rising star. His dramatic and very public arrival in mid-day at the gates of the Agency's Headquarters and his compelling story of survival had made that outcome inevitable.

Daniel and the others had convinced Jake that this was the role he was born to play. The part of the perfect employee, willing and ready to stab his less-than-stellar employer in the back . . . And all for the sake of his lover and her people.

Jake smiled and drained his goblet, accepting another glass of wine from a passing waiter. While he was in the Have Zone, he decided he might as well enjoy himself.

The buffet in the dining room emanated mouth-watering aromas. Jake headed toward the food slowly, nodding his appreciation as various Authority paper pushers and their spouses congratulated him on his daring escape from hell.

At the long table covered with food — more than a family of three could eat in a month — a hostess bragged that the food was organic, supplied by one of their *dealers* from outside the Zones.

"Delicious," Jake mumbled between bites of berry compote. "The raspberries are so tart but perfectly blended with the sweetness of the blueberries. Absolutely perfect."

"They are, aren't they?" she replied, blushing.

Jake chuckled to himself. If only his deluded hostess realized that what she considered a wasteland or *hell* was the birthplace of the heavenly spread before them.

"Agent, that stunt should have cost you your job," Jake's supervisor informed him several hours after his talk show performance aired. "Fortunately for you, the leadership agreed this Goodwill Tour has immense PR value, so you'll get to keep your position — for now."

"Understood, sir." Jake formally saluted, turned around,

and exited the dark wood-paneled office. Returning via the slow route to his small cubicle on a lower floor, he smiled to himself. *I got that old goat by the horns now. He's never liked me, never thought I'd go anywhere because I came from nothing. We'll see if he survives the next Turn Over.*

From the approving looks all others in the building gave Jake, he knew he must be on the right track.

"You're traveling with our beloved leader and his closest inner circle on this tour?" one of Jake's fellow cube farm prisoners asked as Jake sat down at his desk.

He nodded. "Yes, it does sound that way. After all, I know the lay of the land and have conversed with many of the locals."

"Good luck with it." The questioning agent crossed his arms. "You remember your recent history, don't you? The Turn Over began the day the trusting idiots outside the Have Zones were welcomed with bombs falling from our current leader's plane instead of his planned visit."

"Yes, but this time it will be different," Jake replied. "This time, it will end a cold war, not start a new war."

"Such an optimist." The man shook his head and walked away.

Jake sighed. *At the very least, it might start a war that cannot be won by bombs alone.*

The weeks leading up to the leader's goodwill tour had Jake alternating between excitement and dread. There was much to arrange and avoid disclosing as he discretely gathered intelligence and disseminated it to other Protectors working in the Have Not Zones. The PR stop at the former airport outside of Gentle Acres would be made by the Authority's best airship. It was planned to last for approximately fifteen minutes, but a lot could happen in a quarter-hour.

In fact, the Protectors' *gift* needed less than thirty seconds to deliver its intended result. Jake understood and accepted the odds. He was ready to risk his life for the mission — the first mission in his career he had freely chosen to perform and not one that had been thrust upon him.

It was up to him to see it succeed. It was up to him to survive it, if at all possible.

It was up to him to leave some measure of comfort to Zonta if he did not.

You'll know what became of me, Zonta, because I'll have one of Daniel's operatives deliver my letter to you if I don't return after this mission. You will know where my body lies. And you will know the precise spot where to mourn me. I won't let you remain forever in misery, never knowing if or when I'll return to you. You'll enjoy the serenity of closure.

CHAPTER FOURTEEN

Zonta watched as Ryan bent over the old recording device that Mac had built from the scraps of dozens of other scavenged appliances and hit the *play* button. With a whir and buzz, the old-style machine came to life, and a blurry image came into focus on the monitor.

"We thought you might like to see this." Ryan smiled wildly, like a leprechaun salivating over a pot of gold.

"Sorry if the quality isn't very good," Mac explained. "We normally just scan through the Zones' broadcasts for news about what's happening with our friends and family members and don't keep the recordings any of it. But when we saw a commercial about who was going to be on this talk show . . . Well, it speaks for itself."

Zonta nodded slowly and concentrated on the video. A large woman with an even larger mouth gabbed inanely about nothing for a full five minutes until . . .

"Our next guest is Agent Jake Gunderson, a survivor of a horrific ordeal in the hinterlands, which happened outside the safety of the Zones. He'll be attending to our gracious leader's security on the upcoming Unity Tour. Such a brilliant idea of our leader, is it not, Agent Gunderson?"

"It most certainly is."

As the camera pulled back for a two-shot, Zonta's eyes widened. Jake sat in an overstuffed chair next to the hostess. He beamed a shit-eating grin larger than she had thought any human was capable of producing.

"It's a brilliant idea that will bring our lost brothers and sisters into the loving arms of the Authority once and for all." Jake fluttered his eyelashes at his bewitched interviewer. "We will be able to see old friends and family members who chose to stay outside the Zones once again and without the need for checkpoints and security forces."

Zonta gasped. *This is what he's been up to all these weeks? He's trying to recreate the friggin' United Nations?* "What a line of bullshit," she muttered. "He doesn't believe any of what he's saying. That cheesy grin gives him away."

Ryan laughed heartily. "That's what I thought, too. Didn't you say you thought he was flirting big-time with that old broad to cover up his real intentions, Mac?"

"Yep." Mac stroked his chin thoughtfully. "He's putting on a mighty good show for the cameras. Maybe he took some acting lessons in the Agency Academy?"

Zonta frowned. *Acting lessons? Was Jake acting before when he was with me, or is he acting for this dimwitted talk show hostess? Which time is just an* act *for him?*

After the short interview, Ryan switched off the video machine and turned to her. "What do you think?"

"I . . . I don't know. This has got to be some piece of the larger puzzle, but far be it from me to figure out how it all works together."

"But the Fat Man—the bastard's coming here." Mac grimaced. "He's not someone I want to see in the flesh."

"Me neither," Zonta agreed.

She rose from her seat, thanked Ryan and Mac for their kindness, and made an excuse to hurry back to her work. She needed time alone to process through the various parts of the Protectors' plan that she already knew with this latest revelation.

As Zonta turned the corner, an icy chill enveloped her, filling her with dread. Even without quite understanding how all the parts fitted together, she could only conclude that Jake's life was in great danger, now more than ever.

Zonta spied Daphne upon entering the garden. The shapely redhead was working near the large adobe oven that stood beside the fire pit. She and some of the grade-school-aged children were baking bread as part of their practical science cooking class. Zonta switched her trajectory without a thought and headed straight toward her.

Daphne smiled at Zonta's approach and adjusted her lesson accordingly.

"Good job! We'll let your loaves rest and rise some more before we put them in to bake." She turned and winked at Zonta. "Say hello to Ms. Zonta, everyone."

"Hello, Ms. Zonta!" the children sang out.

"Why don't you all go over and help Ms. Elise weed in the root vegetable beds while your loaves are resting?" Zonta suggested, pointing to her assistant and receiving a welcoming nod in return. "Elise looks like she'd really appreciate the help."

The children scrambled and ran toward the nearby plot. Playing in the dirt was always fun at their age, so it was a great way to keep them busy while she grilled Daphne on what she knew of their local Protectors' plans.

"I already know what you want to ask me." Daphne tossed a few more logs into the fire to increase the oven temperature for the baking. "Mac and Ryan told me about the interview earlier today. I stopped by to drop off a few odd tech parts I found in an old hidey-hole in our apartment building's basement."

"So, you know all about this so-called *goodwill tour*?" Zonta took a step closer and lowered her volume. "Do you think it's the ultimate target for Daniel's *kaboom*?"

Daphne wiped the sweat off her brow with the back of her hand and stoked the fire. "Your guess is as good as mine. Daniel is sworn to secrecy. He's never divulged any Protectors' plans in all the years we've been together — off and on. Mostly off, I might add."

"I get it. He's not one to share much of himself unless you prod him, and even then . . ." Zonta shrugged. "From what I've heard, they take some sort of vow to kill any Protector that leaks anything that could bring down their cell."

Daphne rolled her eyes. "Yeah, that sort of pre-Turn Over melodrama would appeal to Daniel." She chuckled nervously. "He's a good person at heart, though. He doesn't want me to be implicated in anything he does, but it's never too hard to put together the pieces. I'm pretty sure that's why he was eager to recruit your Jake into his cell—to gain more information on the Fat Man's future whereabouts."

Zonta frowned. "Did he ever mention anything about what Jake's part was to be in this operation?"

Daphne shook her head. "When he came back in the skirt, I figured that meant they'd been in Zones. Maybe that's when they left Jake there? Daniel often dresses as his old self to go into the Zones. He says the fascists don't pay much attention to a skinny chick with poor fashion sense. It makes it easier for him to get in and out."

Zonta sighed. "I got ya, but why . . . why did Daniel let Jake go back? Surely Daniel realizes what an asset Jake could be for them living on the outside telling them what all he knows of the Agency's operations than the other way around."

Daphne shrugged. "Who knows? The cell must have decided it was worth the risk. Maybe it has something to do with their timetable being pushed forward?"

"Maybe." Zonta bit her lip pensively. Time was never on her side when it came to protecting the men she loved.

If I hadn't been in a rush to do other things the day David wanted to stay on campus and protest, I would have been with him when the militia opened fire and the bombs fell. Now Jake is rushing into something that could mean the death of us all . . . Certain death for him when they realize he's a traitor to the Authority.

Daphne bent over to feel the heat from the oven and then

fed it a few more pieces of wood. "Almost hot enough." She straightened up. "Oh, Daniel did mention something about being able to see an end to the Fat Man's rule sooner rather than later, but I thought it was just so much wishful thinking. After all, the Fat Man's been in charge of the Authority for a very long time. He's survived several coup attempts that we know of and probably a few more that we don't. He's practically indestructible."

"With the Fat Man coming out of his high castle and touring his remote realms, it does sound like the end could be in sight. But where will that leave us?" Zonta wrapped her arms about her middle and paced about the fire pit area. "The Authority isn't going to take too kindly to us tree-planters starting an actual war with them this time out."

"No, they appreciated how docile and complacent we acted a couple decades ago. Just step on us like ants and take power without facing anything scarier than a few protest signs and chants." Daphne snorted. "This . . . *kaboom* is going to wake them up to our actual threat potential and make them *very* cranky with us."

Zonta closed her eyes. *And then the bombs start falling again.* She shuddered. Her friend crossed to her side and hugged her.

"I . . . I don't know if I can take another round of bombings," Zonta whispered. "It was hard to lose David that way. I don't want to see all that we've worked for at Gentle Acres destroyed. I'd rather not live to see it happen."

"I'm sure Daniel and the others have made plans, so it won't come to that." Daphne squeezed Zonta tightly and then let her go. "We'll survive this and be all the stronger for it."

Zonta frowned at her friend. "How can you be so sure?"

Daphne raised her hands heavenwards and laughed. "Because that's what we women do—we survive and grow stronger with time and experience. Screw the men! They're the ones who cause all the wars and increase the hate. But women will survive because we've got love and an excellent recipe for whole wheat spelt flour bread."

The children came running back to their baking class at that moment, giggling and shouting, their bodies in motion and their hearts in hopeful expectation. The future was assured as long as they had a generation to cherish and protect.

Zonta smiled at Daphne, then at each precious child of Gentle Acres. She hugged them and tousled their hair, then helped them ready their baked goods for the oven.

Within a few minutes, a heavenly aroma filled the air. "Ah, homemade bread and love," Zonta murmured. "They make all the difference."

Two weeks later

Zonta glanced up from the field where she was busily sowing winter wheat. The incessant drone of the aircraft above made the hairs on the back of her neck stand on end. She had never felt quite so hemmed in by the Authority before, trapped in their square of cropland and housing.

The number of aerial patrols had increased daily. If Daniel's group had a secret weapon, it most certainly wasn't going to be a secret for much longer. Why the Agency hadn't sent out men on foot to do a survey of the area before the great leader's airship was to arrive was beyond her. Maybe that was Jake's doing?

Why hasn't Jake returned? Surely they'd want an agent with some familiarity with Gentle Acres to come and check it out before their beloved dictator showed his ugly face, right?

Zonta dipped her hand into the seed bag slung diagonally across her body, sprinkled the seeds into the furrow, and kept walking. It was time for her to be brutally honest—Jake was never returning to Gentle Acres. She would have to relearn how to survive alone once again.

Each step Zonta took across the field became increasingly painful. *They probably tortured Jake and made him reveal the Protectors' plans. They've slung him into prison and executed him. Or, even worse, they turned him back to their ways with a substantial bribe of money or the promise of career advancement. Or maybe he's met a beautiful Have woman who's enticed him into her bed . . .*

Did it matter what had prevented him from returning to her? Life continued. The winter cover crop needed sowing. Zonta forcefully pushed the troubling thoughts from her mind.

"Penny for your thoughts," Jefferson called out from a couple of furrows over.

Zonta had stopped, motionless in her musing. She plastered a grin on her face and turned. "I've always wondered what that expression really meant, especially since we gave up on that particular monetary system a long time ago."

Jefferson chuckled and approached closer. "Yeah, we've got to create some new idioms for the world we currently inhabit. Our dialect is an odd mix of the old times and the present one." He paused and considered her for a moment. "Are you all right?"

"I'm fine," she covered. "Just feeling tired lately, what with the fading autumn light and all. But with our temperatures still in the 80s most days, we've got to make the most of the weather. I'm not even sure we'll need to plant a winter cover crop in a few years. Our mean temps are still going up."

"*Climate change is real*, they used to say." Jefferson looked off to the horizon and sighed. "My former next-door neighbor used to say it over and over like a mantra. I don't know if it was to convince himself, others, or if he believed it was a magic spell that would somehow hold it off."

"Whatever happened to Bob?" Zonta rubbed her lower back. "Ooh, my back is killing me. Wasn't he a chiropractor?"

Jefferson took the seed bag from her shoulder and allowed Zonta to stretch her arms toward the ground and overhead to work out the kink. "Bob ended up being dragged into the Workers' Zone by his daughter-in-law and her family. They wanted him to continue their chiro treatments, and he knew the workers there could use the help."

Jefferson tilted his head and squinted in the late afternoon sunlight. "You know, for a red person, you're looking rather pale. Are you sure you're feeling okay?"

"I've not been eating much. Everything seems to taste . . . off. You think I've caught one of the plagues? We probably haven't been careful enough in our screening of newcomers for signs of infection."

Jefferson shook his head and chuckled. "Uh-huh. I bet this kind of *plague* takes nine months to cure."

Zonta frowned. "That's not funny, Jeff."

"Wasn't meant to be, but I know that look. You forget that once upon a time I was a father."

Jefferson handed Zonta the seed sack and returned to his chores. She looked up at the patrol plane circling overhead, feeling her heartbeat pounding in her ears. She had felt tender spots on her breasts earlier, and her erratic menstrual cycle hadn't begun this month.

Deep down, Zonta knew Jefferson spoke the truth.

Jake was not here, but he would never be far from her.

CHAPTER FIFTEEN

The plan seemed to be going well enough to give Jake a momentary breather. He rose to leave the thick cigar smoke of the leader's cabin to find a seat with the lesser dignitaries on the lower decks away from the airship's top-tier observation windows.

"Is that the primitive utopia you fell in love with, Agent?" an angular woman with a hawkish stare asked before he could slip away. She pointed to the rubble of a city below and gave a sigh of disgust. "Looks like so much trash to me."

Jake gritted his teeth but kept his expression neutral. The cabinet members and their wives were perhaps the most infuriatingly narrow-minded, rude, and callous people he'd ever encountered. Even the leader exhibited better manners most of the time.

"No, that's a different city down there," he replied. "Now, if you'll excuse me—"

"But aren't they more or less alike?" She barred his way to the exit with a bony arm. "Without basic services and the finer things of life, that rubble might as well as be a jungle. And what survives well in the wild? Animals do, of course."

Jake cringed inwardly. "Uh, I think you might be operating under a misconception. We're going to an actual village."

"Oh?" She raised an over-plucked eyebrow and pretended to smile. "Perhaps after we annex these little primitive colonies, we could make them all into wildlife preserves. I know my husband really misses big game hunting. Stupid elephants had to die out before he got a chance to bag one. These primitives might just fill that gap."

Jake couldn't take it anymore. He turned and escaped as the sound of a popping champagne cork momentarily distracted his tormentor.

On the lower decks, things were equally festive. Drinks were being served, and the conversation was more raucous than the elites' sedate droning above. Jake grabbed a beer and found a seat in a relatively empty corner. This gave him time to send a quick signal to the others on the ground, so they could better estimate the arrival time for the airship. He pressed the small square device in his coat pocket and felt a reassuring vibration that it had been sent and received.

Thinking back to just months previous, he realized just how easy it would have been to send a signal via the chip that had been implanted in his neck. But his *accident* had made that impossible. The doctors had declared it was too dangerous for him to ever be chipped again. To say he was relieved would be a gross understatement. He much preferred not being followed, monitored, or killed by remote control.

Why he'd ever believed the Agency wouldn't kill one of their own, he couldn't fathom anymore. It's like he hadn't been fully awake or alive before he'd met Zonta. She'd opened his eyes to the futility of his existence within the Authority. There was no way to move up in a world created to keep the majority down so that a relative few could have whatever they wanted.

About a half-hour later, the pilot's voice came on over the speakers. "Crew, prepare for landing. Passengers, take your seats."

It's now or never. You can do this. You're going to do this. And then you're going to escape this life for good.

Jake slipped out of the compartment and made his way to the lowest level. From there, he would be able to slide down the ropes as the airship approached the runway. He pulled off his jacket and removed his tie. He'd blend in with the ground staff and get far enough away from the airship when the *surprise* arrived so as not to get toasted.

The next ten minutes flashed by in a blur.

Jake went through the steps in his head, ticking each one off his mental list as he completed it. He spotted the trolley on the tarmac that was supposed to whisk the leader and his entourage to a predetermined location at the airfield, a place where the leader would give his remarks in front of bussed-in workers from the closest Have Not Zone. Nothing was to be left to chance for this photo op. The primitives of Gentle Acres and the other farm cooperatives would never behave in the way the press secretary desired for the camera, so loyal Zone workers would have to suffice.

As the airship drifted closer to the ground, Jake spied a small white van—the kind of which hadn't been seen in at least fifty years—pulling alongside the trolley. It had to be Daniel and one of the others with the *surprise*. The timer had only thirty seconds on it once it was set, so the occupants would have to make a mad dash for the fields to safely clear the blast area.

It's time. I'll be with you soon, Zonta.

Jake slipped past a ground crew member and got onto one of the ropes. He lowered himself, hand over hand, making his descent just as an Agency vehicle sped onto the tarmac and opened fire on the white van. The Protectors inside flung open its rear doors and returned fire. The Agency vehicle continued racing toward the van, preparing to ram it.

No! You bastards! It's too soon! Too soon!

Jake felt the shockwave of the explosion and intense heat before the deafening roar reached his ears. Then he found himself falling, falling . . . before he blacked out.

Three weeks later

Jake woke up with a terribly dry mouth and the smell of

burnt hair in his nostrils. He tried focusing his gaze on any-thing in front of him, but he found it difficult to make things out clearly.

What happened to me? Where the hell am I?

"Don't try to move. You're healing. It's good to see you're still with us." A soft tenor voice sounded close.

Jake turned his head slowly toward the voice. He blinked, and his blurry vision sharpened. He discovered the voice be-longed to a young man wrapped in a green cap, mask, and scrubs. *Am I in a hospital?*

Jake blinked again. "Am I . . . alive?"

"Yeah, and it's a miracle. You're one of only a handful of survivors of the airship crash. We got you transferred to the closest Workers' Zone med clinic. Luckily for you, you've missed much of the bloodshed from these past few days after the leader and his cabinet secretaries met with early ends."

The plan was a success after all? Daniel did say they had more than enough nitrate fertilizer to take out the airship, if not the entire airport.

"The Fat Man is gone?" he whispered. "The Authority is . . ."

"Is no more." The nurse finished his sentence. "Rest now and dream sweet dreams. Things are looking up. At least for us lowly Have Nots, it's looking better. The border walls and security checkpoints have all been pulled down. The people are taking back what was stolen from them by the Haves. By the time your skin has healed, it will be an entirely new world outside these doors."

Jake tried to smile, but it hurt too much. His eyes fluttered close at the exertion.

A new world. Dream sweet dreams. Sweet dreams of Zonta.

CHAPTER SIXTEEN

Zonta rose early. A heavy dew had condensed on the empty fields, with patches of light frost dotting the landscape as the weary sun peeked over the horizon. Only the cold-tolerant crops were growing now. The fading annuals had long since been cleared away to be burned and composted.

Strolling through the gardens, Zonta considered how she'd always found solace in the late autumn, a time when nature enjoyed a brief respite before the full bitterness of winter set in. Of course, winter lasted for a much shorter period now than it had when she was a child, thanks to the build-up of carbon dioxide in the atmosphere and the rising mean temperature. But it was just as harsh, if not more so, while it lasted.

After this first cold spell, they'd probably see some warmer days before the first real blizzard. Their greenhouse produce was sprouting profusely, so fresh spinach and kale wouldn't be too long now. She salivated at the thought. She has had a real craving for greens lately.

Zonta patted her belly and sat on a low bench beside the orchard's entrance. She'd learn from the midwife this week that her baby would be born in the spring. This revelation meant she'd have to hand over the majority of the garden's direction this coming growing season to Elise and Jenna.

She had no fears — the two newest master gardeners were more than up to the task. It was the letting go of the power she held as the garden director she wondered about. Could she hand over the keys to the kingdom graciously and not be tempted to meddle or second-guess their decisions?

It was going to be a challenging year at Gentle Acres. Their small community was growing, and not just because of births. Refugees from the Zones were even now straggling into their cooperatives, looking for their loved ones, searching for a different life, hungry for freedom and for food.

The faint snap of a twig and a rustle of dried grass caused Zonta to turn her head.

"Who's there?" she called out.

No answer. There were relatively few walkers in the gardens so early at this time of the year. Her heartburn and disrupted sleep pattern had made her an early riser. *It must have been a rabbit or a groundhog.*

The sun rose higher into the sky, and the morning birds began to sing. There was work to be done. Zonta knew she couldn't sit around all day, so she stood and began to walk toward her office. Two steps later, something inside her told her to turn around and walk through the orchard instead.

Zonta had avoided strolling through the trees for far too long. The last time she had visited the orchard was the day of the big explosion. The sound and vibrations of Daniel's *kaboom* had rattled windows all throughout Gentle Acres and its environs. The dense smoke had been visible from the rooftops and second stories.

Zonta had been lying beneath the apple tree where she and Jake had lain that fateful day their baby had been conceived. Brilliant flames arced across the sky. She knew instinctively that Jake was on the airship, certain he had been killed instantly or mortally wounded.

A letter written by Jake had been given to her the next day, solemnly handed over by one of the Protectors who had stayed behind to manage communications. Zonta knew what the note meant. She didn't have the heart to read it just then, so she'd carefully placed it into her desk drawer for safekeeping.

Zonta had found it too painful to return to their special spot until now. The memories were too fresh, but the growing reminder within her of Jake's love had helped mend her broken heart. She had never enjoyed such a distraction after David's disappearance, and it seemed to have prolonged her mourning. Now she had someone to live for and a task to focus on. Thinking about her child's future kept recent events in perspective.

Zonta reached the tree and sat down at its base. Her worn jeans weren't enough to keep her warm on the cold, damp ground. After a few minutes, she stood up and brushed off her backside. A sudden *snap* behind her grabbed her attention. She spun around.

The autumn sunlight slanted through the mostly bare tree limbs. Zonta spotted a shadow moving at the end of the row.

She took a step closer and squinted. She could just make out a slightly bent figure standing at the end of the row. It leaned heavily on a cane then limped toward her.

Zonta's heart leapt.

"Jake? Is it you?"

"Yes," came a gravelly voice, strained yet familiar.

She gasped. Was she dreaming? "It's *really* you?"

"Yes, it's really me — or what's left of me." Jake paused and took a deep breath. "A lot of me got practically incinerated, but I'm healing. They said I could go home, and this is where I wanted to go. I'm home at last . . . with you."

Zonta sobbed. "Yes, you are."

She held out her arms and walked into the long-desired embrace of her lover.

ABOUT THE AUTHOR

Cindy A. Matthews is a freelance writer/editor and novelist. She edits *The Revolution Continues,* a blog covering topics ranging from climate change and the environment to social issues and movements such as *Black Lives Matter* and *Medicare For All.* A challenge to create a dystopian love story during the middle of the COVID-19 lockdown inspired her to write *Where The Bodies Lie.*

Cindy grew up reading science fiction classics along with thousands of romances. She co-writes The BloodDark series with her husband, Adrian J. Matthews. She writes contemporary and fantasy romantic comedies as Cynthianna. She writes SF/vampire erotic romance under the pen name of Celine Chatillon. You can learn more about her fiction and non-fiction at her websites:

cindyamatthews.com
cynthianna.com
celinechatillon.com
blooddarkbooks.blogspot.com
therevolutioncontinues.com

In her free time, Cindy likes to organic garden, sing in a band, attend SF cons, and help immigrants deal with the confusing labyrinth of the US immigration system.

www.ingramcontent.com/pod-product-compliance
Lightning Source LLC
Chambersburg PA
CBHW070755120626
46557CB00002B/614